The Fox

"The greatest imaginative novelist of our generation."
E.M. Forster

"Lawrence, who brought to consciousness and formulated so
much that was coming to life in the country as a whole, is
blended into the cultural air we breathe. It is not easy to know
what is our own, and what came through him."
Ted Hughes

"The greatest writer of the century."
Philip Larkin

"He's an intoxicator... Has there ever been anyone like him
for bringing places and people so vividly to life?"
Doris Lessing

ONEWORLD CLASSICS

The Fox

D.H. Lawrence

ONEWORLD
CLASSICS

ONEWORLD CLASSICS LTD
London House
243-253 Lower Mortlake Road
Richmond
Surrey TW9 2LL
United Kingdom
www.oneworldclassics.com

The Fox first published in 1923
This edition first published by Oneworld Classics Limited in 2009
Notes and background material © Oneworld Classics Ltd, 2009

Printed in Great Britain by CPI Antony Rowe

ISBN: 978-1-84749-096-4

Contents

D.H. Lawrence (1885–1930)

Lydia Lawrence,
D.H. Lawrence's mother

Ernest Lawrence,
D.H. Lawrence's brother

Jessie Chambers

Frieda Lawrence

Nottingham Road, Eastwood, *c*.1900. D.H. Lawrence was
born in Victoria Street, off this main road, on the right

D.H. Lawrence's birthplace
in Victoria Street, Eastwood

The chapel designed to house
D.H. Lawrence's ashes

Tuesday

Now I can't stand it any longer, I can't. For two hours I have n't moved a muscle — just sat and thought. — ~~and I~~ I have written a letter to Ernst. You need n't, of course, send it. But you must say to him all I have said. No more dishonour, no more lies. Let them do their — silliest — but no more subterfuge, lying, dirt, fear. I feel as if it would strangle me. What is it all but procrastination? No, I can't bear it, because it's bad. I love you. Let us face anything, do anything, put up with anything. But this crawling under the mud I cannot bear.

I'm afraid I've got a fit of heroics. I've tried so hard to work — but I can't. This situation is round my chest like a cord. It mustn't continue. I will go right away, if you like. I will stop in Metz till you get Ernst's answer to the truth. But no, I won't utter or act or willingly let you utter or act, another single lie in the business.

I'm not going to joke, I'm not going to laugh, I'm not going to make light of things for you. The situation tortures me too much. It's the situation, the situation I can't stand — no, and I won't. I love you too much.

Don't show this letter to either of your sisters — no. Let us be good. You are clean, but you dirty your feet. I'll sign myself as you call me — ~~Mr Lawrence~~ — and then, I say, that I love you

Lawrence's letter to Frieda Weekley,
7th May 1912

The Fox

THE TWO GIRLS were usually known by their surnames, Banford and March. They had taken the farm together, intending to work it all by themselves: that is, they were going to rear chickens, make a living by poultry and add to this by keeping a cow and raising one or two young beasts. Unfortunately things did not turn out well.

Banford was a small, thin, delicate thing with spectacles. She, however, was the principal investor, for March had little or no money. Banford's father, who was a tradesman in Islington, gave his daughter the start for her health's sake, and because he loved her, and because it did not look as if she would marry. March was more robust. She had learnt carpentry and joinery at the evening classes in Islington. She would be the man about the place. They had, moreover, Banford's old grandfather living with them at the start. He had been a farmer. But unfortunately the old man died after he had been at Bailey Farm for a year. Then the two girls were left alone.

They were neither of them young: that is, they were near thirty. But they certainly were not old. They set out quite gallantly with their enterprise. They had numbers of chickens, black Leghorns and white Leghorns, Plymouths and Wyandottes; also some ducks; also two heifers in the fields. One heifer unfortunately refused absolutely to stay in the Bailey Farm closes. No matter how March made up the fences, the heifer was out, wild in the woods, or trespassing on the neighbouring pasture, and March and Banford were away, flying after her, with more haste than success. So this heifer they sold in despair. Then, just before the other beast was expecting her first calf, the old man died, and the girls, afraid of the coming event, sold her in a panic, and limited their attentions to fowls and ducks.

In spite of a little chagrin, it was a relief to have no more cattle on hand. Life was not made merely to be slaved away. Both girls agreed in this. The fowls were quite enough trouble. March had set up her carpenter's bench at the end of the open shed. Here she worked, making coops and doors and other appurtenances. The fowls were housed in the bigger building, which had served as barn and cowshed in old days. They had a beautiful home, and should have been perfectly content.

Indeed they looked well enough. But the girls were disgusted at their tendency to strange illnesses, at their exacting way of life and at their refusal – obstinate refusal – to lay eggs.

March did most of the outdoor work. When she was out and about, in her puttees and breeches, her belted coat and her loose cap, she looked almost like some graceful, loose-balanced young man, for her shoulders were straight, and her movements easy and confident, even tinged with a little indifference or irony. But her face was not a man's face, ever. The wisps of her crisp dark hair blew about her as she stooped, her eyes were big and wide and dark, when she looked up again, strange, startled, shy and sardonic at once. Her mouth, too, was almost pinched as if in pain and irony. There was something odd and unexplained about her. She would stand balanced on one hip, looking at the fowls pattering about in the obnoxious fine mud of the sloping yard, and calling to her favourite white hen, which came in answer to her name. But there was an almost satirical flicker in March's big, dark eyes as she looked at her three-toed flock pottering about under her gaze, and the same slight dangerous satire in her voice as she spoke to the favoured Patty, who pecked at March's boot by way of friendly demonstration.

Fowls did not flourish at Bailey Farm, in spite of all that March did for them. When she provided hot food for them in the morning, according to rule, she noticed that it made them heavy and dozy for hours. She expected to see them lean against the pillars of the shed in their languid processes of digestion. And she knew quite well that they ought to be busily scratching and foraging about if they were to come to any good. So she decided to give them their hot food at night, and let them sleep on it. Which she did. But it made no difference.

War conditions, again, were very unfavourable to poultry-keeping. Food was scarce and bad. And when the Daylight Saving Bill was passed, the fowls obstinately refused to go to bed, as usual, about nine o'clock in the summertime. That was late enough, indeed, for there was no peace till they were shut up and asleep. Now they cheerfully walked around, without so much as glancing at the barn, until ten o'clock or later. Both Banford and March disbelieved in living for work alone. They wanted to read or take a cycle ride in the evening, or perhaps March wished to paint curvilinear swans on porcelain, with green background, or else make a marvellous fire screen by processes of elaborate cabinet-work. For she was a creature of odd whims and unsatisfied tendencies. But from all these things she was prevented by the stupid fowls.

One evil there was greater than any other. Bailey Farm was a little homestead, with ancient wooden barn and two-gabled farmhouse, lying just one field removed from the edge of the wood. Since the War the fox was a demon. He carried off the hens under the very noses of March and Banford. Banford would start and stare through her big spectacles with all her eyes, as another squawk and flutter took place at her heels. Too late! Another white Leghorn gone. It was disheartening.

They did what they could to remedy it. When it became permitted to shoot foxes, they stood sentinel with their guns, the two of them, at the favoured hours. But it was no good. The fox was too quick for them. So another year passed, and another, and they were living on their losses, as Banford said. They let their farmhouse one summer, and retired to live in a railway carriage that was deposited as a sort of outhouse in a corner of the field. This amused them, and helped their finances. Nonetheless, things looked dark.

Although they were usually the best of friends, because Banford, though nervous and delicate, was a warm, generous soul, and March, though so odd and absent in herself, had a strange magnanimity, yet in the long solitude they were apt to become a little irritable with one another, tired of one another. March had four fifths of the work to do, and though she did not mind, there seemed no relief, and it made her eyes flash curiously sometimes. Then Banford, feeling more nerve-worn than ever, would become despondent, and March would speak sharply to her. They seemed to be losing ground somehow, losing hope as the months went by. There alone in the fields by the wood, with the wide country stretching hollow and dim to the round hills of the White Horse in the far distance, they seemed to have to live too much off themselves. There was nothing to keep them up – and no hope.

The fox really exasperated them both. As soon as they had let the fowls out in the early summer mornings they had to take their guns and keep guard – and then again, as soon as evening began to mellow, they must go once more. And he was so sly. He slid along in the deep grass; he was difficult as a serpent to see. And he seemed to circumvent the girls deliberately. Once or twice March had caught sight of the white tip of his brush, or the ruddy shadow of him in the deep grass, and she had let fire at him. But he made no account of this.

One evening March was standing with her back to the sunset, her gun under her arm, her hair pushed under her cap. She was half watching, half musing. It was her constant state. Her eyes were keen and observant, but her inner mind took no notice of what she saw. She was always lapsing into this odd, rapt state, her mouth rather screwed up. It was a question whether she was there, actually consciously present, or not.

The trees on the wood edge were a darkish, brownish green in the full light – for it was the end of August. Beyond, the naked, copper-like shafts and limbs of the pine trees shone in the air. Nearer, the rough grass, with its long brownish stalks all agleam, was full of light. The fowls were round about – the ducks were still swimming on the pond under the pine trees. March looked at it all, saw it all and did not see it. She heard Banford speaking to the fowls in the distance, and she did not hear. What was she thinking about? Heaven knows. Her consciousness was, as it were, held back.

She lowered her eyes, and suddenly saw the fox. He was looking up at her. His chin was pressed down, and his eyes were looking up. They met her eyes. And he knew her. She was spellbound – she knew he knew her. So he looked into her eyes, and her soul failed her. He knew her, he was not daunted.

She struggled, confusedly she came to herself, and saw him making off, with slow leaps over some fallen boughs – slow, impudent jumps. Then he glanced over his shoulder, and ran smoothly away. She saw his brush held smooth like a feather, she saw his white buttocks twinkle. And he was gone softly, soft as the wind.

She put her gun to her shoulder, but even then pursed her mouth, knowing it was nonsense to pretend to fire. So she began to walk slowly after him, in the direction he had gone, slowly, pertinaciously. She expected to find him. In her heart she was determined to find him. What she would do when she saw him again she did not consider. But she was determined to find him. So she walked abstractedly about on the edge of the wood, with wide, vivid dark eyes, and a faint flush in her cheeks. She did not think. In strange mindlessness she walked hither and thither.

At last she became aware that Banford was calling her. She made an effort of attention, turned, and gave some sort of screaming call in answer. Then again she was striding off towards the homestead. The red sun was setting, the fowls were retiring towards their roost. She watched them, white creatures, black creatures, gathering to the barn. She watched them spellbound, without seeing them. But her automatic intelligence told her when it was time to shut the door.

She went indoors to supper, which Banford had set on the table. Banford chatted easily. March seemed to listen, in her distant, manly way. She answered a brief word now and then. But all the time she was as if spellbound. And as soon as supper was over, she rose again to go out, without saying why.

She took her gun again and went to look for the fox. For he had lifted his eyes upon her, and his knowing look seemed to have entered her brain. She did not so much think of him – she was possessed by him. She saw his dark, shrewd, unabashed eye looking into her, knowing her. She felt him invisibly master her spirit. She knew the way he lowered his chin as he looked up, she knew his muzzle, the golden brown and the greyish white. And again she saw him glance over his shoulder at her, half inviting, half contemptuous and cunning. So she went, with her great startled eyes glowing, her gun under her arm, along the wood edge. Meanwhile the night fell, and a great moon rose above the pine trees. And again Banford was calling.

So she went indoors. She was silent and busy. She examined her gun and cleaned it, musing abstractedly by the lamplight. Then she went out again, under the great moon, to see if everything was right. When she saw the dark crests of the pine trees against the blood-red sky, again her heart beat to the fox, the fox. She wanted to follow him with her gun.

It was some days before she mentioned the affair to Banford. Then suddenly, one evening she said:

"The fox was right at my feet on Saturday night."

"Where?" said Banford, her eyes opening behind her spectacles.

"When I stood just above the pond."

"Did you fire?" cried Banford.

"No, I didn't."

"Why not?"

"Why, I was too much surprised, I suppose."

It was the same old, slow, laconic way of speech March always had. Banford stared at her friend for a few moments.

"You saw him?" she cried.

7

"Oh yes! He was looking up at me, cool as anything."

"I tell you," cried Banford, "the cheek! They're not afraid of us, Nellie."

"Oh, no," said March.

"Pity you didn't get a shot at him," said Banford.

"Isn't it a pity! I've been looking for him ever since. But I don't suppose he'll come so near again."

"I don't suppose he will," said Banford.

And she proceeded to forget about it, except that she was more indignant than ever at the impudence of the beggars. March was also not conscious that she thought of the fox. But whenever she fell into her half-musing, when she was half rapt, and half-intelligently aware of what passed under her vision, then it was the fox which somehow dominated her unconsciousness, possessed the blank half of her musing. And so it was for weeks and months. No matter whether she had been climbing the trees for the apples, or beating down the last of the damsons, or whether she had been digging out the ditch from the duck pond, or clearing out the barn when she had finished, or when she had straightened herself, and pushed the wisps of hair away again from her forehead, and pursed up her mouth again in an odd, screwed fashion, much too old for her years, there was sure to come over her mind the old spell of the fox, as it came when he was looking at her. It was as if she could smell him at these times. And it always recurred at unexpected moments, just as she was going to sleep at night, or just as she was pouring the water into the teapot to make tea – it was the fox, it came over her like a spell.

So the months passed. She still looked for him unconsciously when she went towards the wood. He had become a settled effect in her spirit, a state permanently established, not continuous, but always recurring. She did not know what she felt or thought – only the state came over her, as when he looked at her.

The months passed, the dark evenings came – heavy, dark November, when March went about in high boots, ankle-deep in mud, when the night began to fall at four o'clock, and the day never properly dawned. Both girls dreaded these times. They dreaded the almost continuous darkness that enveloped them on their desolate little farm near the wood. Banford was physically afraid. She was afraid of tramps, afraid lest someone should come prowling around. March was not so much afraid as uncomfortable and disturbed. She felt discomfort and gloom in all her physique.

Usually the two girls had tea in the sitting room. March lit a fire at dusk, and put on the wood she had chopped and sawed during the day. Then the long evening was in front: dark, sodden, black outside; lonely and rather oppressive inside, a little dismal. March was content not to talk, but Banford could not keep still. Merely listening to the wind in the pines outside, or the drip of water, was too much for her.

One evening the girls had washed up the tea things in the kitchen, and March had put on her house shoes, and taken up a roll of crochet-work, which she worked at slowly from time to time. So she lapsed into silence. Banford stared at the red fire which, being of wood, needed constant attention. She was afraid to begin to read too early, because her eyes would not bear any strain. So she sat staring at the fire, listening to the distant sounds – sound of cattle lowing, of a dull, heavy moist wind, of the rattle of the evening train on the little railway not far off. She was almost fascinated by the red glow of the fire.

Suddenly both girls started and lifted their heads. They heard a footstep – distinctly a footstep. Banford recoiled in fear. March stood listening. Then rapidly she approached the door that led into the kitchen. At the same time they heard the footsteps approach the back door. They waited a second. The back door opened softly. Banford gave a loud cry. A man's voice said softly:

"Hello!"

March recoiled, and took a gun from a corner.

"What do you want?" she cried, in a sharp voice.

Again the soft, softly vibrating man's voice said:

"Hello! What's wrong?"

"I shall shoot!" cried March. "What do you want?"

"Why, what's wrong? What's wrong?" came the soft, wondering, rather scared voice, and a young soldier, with his heavy kit on his back, advanced into the dim light.

"Why," he said, "who lives here then?"

"We live here," said March. "What do you want?"

"Oh!" came the long, melodious, wonder note from the young soldier. "Doesn't William Grenfel live here then?"

"No – you know he doesn't."

"Do I? Do I? I don't, you see. He *did* live here, because he was my grandfather, and I lived here myself five years ago. What's become of him then?"

The young man – or youth, for he would not be more than twenty, now advanced and stood in the inner doorway. March, already under the influence of his strange, soft, modulated voice, stared at him spellbound. He had a ruddy, roundish face, with fairish hair, rather long, flattened to his forehead with sweat. His eyes were blue, and very bright and sharp. On his cheeks, on the fresh ruddy skin were fine, fair hairs, like a down, but sharper. It gave him a slightly glistening look. Having his heavy sack on his shoulders, he stooped, thrusting his head forwards. His hat was loose in one hand. He stared brightly, very keenly from girl to girl, particularly at March, who stood pale, with great dilated eyes, in her belted coat and puttees, her hair knotted in a big crisp knot behind. She still had the gun in her hand. Behind her, Banford, clinging to the sofa arm, was shrinking away, with half-averted head.

"I thought my grandfather still lived here? I wonder if he's dead."

"We've been here for three years," said Banford, who was beginning to recover her wits, seeing something boyish in the round head with its rather long, sweaty hair.

"Three years! You don't say so! And you don't know who was here before you?"

"I know it was an old man who lived by himself."

"Ay! Yes, that's him! And what became of him then?"

"He died. I know he died…"

"Ay! He's dead then!"

The youth stared at them without changing colour or expression. If he had any expression, besides a slight baffled look of wonder, it was one of sharp curiosity concerning the two girls – sharp, impersonal curiosity, the curiosity of that round young head.

But to March, he was the fox. Whether it was the thrusting forward of his head, or the glisten of fine whitish hairs on the ruddy cheekbones, or the bright, keen eyes, that can never be said – but the boy was to her the fox, and she could not see him otherwise.

"How was it you didn't know if your grandfather was alive or dead?" asked Banford, recovering her natural sharpness.

"Ay, that's it," replied the softly breathing youth. "You see, I joined up in Canada, and I hadn't heard for three or four years. I ran away to Canada."

"And now have you just come from France?"

"Well – from Salonika really."

There was a pause, nobody knowing quite what to say.

"So you've nowhere to go now?" said Banford rather lamely.

"Oh, I know some people in the village. Anyhow, I can go to the Swan."

"You came on the train, I suppose. Would you like to sit down a bit?"

"Well – I don't mind."

He gave an odd little groan as he swung off his kit. Banford looked at March.

"Put the gun down," she said. "We'll make a cup of tea."

"Ay," said the youth. "We've seen enough of rifles."

He sat down rather tired on the sofa, leaning forwards.

March recovered her presence of mind, and went into the kitchen. There she heard the soft young voice musing:

"Well, to think I should come back and find it like this!" He did not seem sad, not at all – only rather interestedly surprised.

"And what a difference in the place, eh?" he continued, looking round the room.

"You see a difference, do you?" said Banford.

"Yes – don't I!"

His eyes were unnaturally clear and bright, though it was the brightness of abundant health.

March was busy in the kitchen preparing another meal. It was about seven o'clock. All the time, while she was active, she was attending to the youth in the sitting room, not so much listening to what he said, as feeling the soft run of his voice. She primmed up her mouth tighter and tighter, puckering it as if it were sewed, in her effort to keep her will uppermost. Yet her large eyes dilated and glowed in spite of her; she lost herself. Rapidly and carelessly she prepared the meal, cutting large chunks of bread and margarine – for there was no butter. She racked her brain to think of something else to put on the tray – she had only bread, margarine and jam, and the larder was bare. Unable to conjure anything up, she went into the sitting room with her tray.

She did not want to be noticed. Above all, she did not want him to look at her. But when she came in, and was busy setting the table just behind him, he pulled himself up from his sprawling, and turned and looked over his shoulder. She became pale and wan.

The youth watched her as she bent over the table, looked at her slim, well-shapen legs, at the belted coat, dropping around her thighs, at the knot of dark hair, and his curiosity, vivid and widely alert, was again arrested by her.

The lamp was shaded with a dark-green shade so that the light was thrown downwards, the upper half of the room was dim. His face moved bright under the light, but March loomed shadowy in the distance.

She turned round, but kept her eyes sideways, dropping and lifting her dark lashes. Her mouth unpuckered as she said to Banford, "Will you pour out?"

Then she went into the kitchen again.

"Have your tea where you are, will you?" said Banford to the youth. "Unless you'd rather come to the table."

"Well," said he, "I'm nice and comfortable here, aren't I? I will have it here, if you don't mind."

"There's nothing but bread and jam," she said. And she put his plate on a stool by him. She was very happy now, waiting on him. For she loved company. And now she was no more afraid of him than if he were her own younger brother. He was such a boy.

"Nellie," she called. "I've poured you a cup out."

March appeared in the doorway, took her cup and sat down in a corner, as far from the light as possible. She was very sensitive in her knees. Having no skirts to cover them, and being forced to sit with them boldly exposed, she suffered. She shrank and shrank, trying not to be seen. And the youth, sprawling low on the couch, glanced up at her, with long, steady, penetrating looks, till she was almost ready to disappear. Yet she held her cup balanced, she drank her tea, screwed up her mouth and held her head averted. Her desire to be invisible was so strong that it quite baffled the youth. He felt he could not see her distinctly. She seemed like a shadow within the shadow. And ever his eyes came back to her, searching, unremitting, with unconscious fixed attention.

Meanwhile he was talking softly and smoothly to Banford, who loved nothing so much as gossip, and who was full of perky interest, like a bird. Also he ate largely and quickly and voraciously, so that March had to cut more chunks of bread and margarine, for the roughness of which Banford apologized.

"Oh, well," said March, suddenly speaking, "if there's no butter to put on it, it's no good trying to make dainty pieces."

Again the youth watched her, and he laughed, with a sudden, quick laugh, showing his teeth and wrinkling his nose.

"It isn't, is it," he answered in his soft, near voice.

It appeared he was Cornish by birth and upbringing. When he was twelve years old he had come to Bailey Farm with his grandfather, with whom he had never agreed very well. So he had run away to Canada, and worked far away in the west. Now he was here – and that was the end of it.

He was very curious about the girls, to find out exactly what they were doing. His questions were those of a farm youth – acute, practical, a little mocking. He was very much amused by their attitude to their losses – for they were amusing on the score of heifers and fowls.

"Oh, well," broke in March, "we don't believe in living for nothing but work."

"Don't you?" he answered. And again the quick young laugh came over his face. He kept his eyes steadily on the obscure woman in the corner.

"But what will you do when you've used up all your capital?" he said.

"Oh, I don't know," answered March laconically. "Hire ourselves out for land workers, I suppose."

"Yes, but there won't be any demand for women land workers now the War's over," said the youth.

"Oh, we'll see. We shall hold on a bit longer yet," said March, with a plangent, half-sad, half-ironical indifference.

"There wants a man about the place," said the youth softly. Banford burst out laughing.

"Take care what you say," she interrupted. "We consider ourselves quite efficient."

"Oh," came March's slow, plangent voice, "it isn't a case of efficiency, I'm afraid. If you're going to do farming you must be at it from morning till night, and you might as well be a beast yourself."

"Yes, that's it," said the youth. "You aren't willing to put yourselves into it."

"We aren't," said March, "and we know it."

"We want some of our time for ourselves," said Banford.

The youth threw himself back on the sofa, his face tight with laughter, and laughed silently but thoroughly. The calm scorn of the girls tickled him tremendously.

"Yes," he said, "but why did you begin then?"

"Oh," said March, "we had a better opinion of the nature of fowls then than we have now."

"Of nature altogether, I'm afraid," said Banford. "Don't talk to me about nature."

Again the face of the youth tightened with delighted laughter. "You haven't a very high opinion of fowls and cattle, have you?" he said.

"Oh no – quite a low one," said March.

He laughed out.

"Neither fowls nor heifers," said Banford, "nor goats nor the weather."

The youth broke into a sharp yap of laughter, delighted. The girls began to laugh too, March turning aside her face and wrinkling her mouth in amusement.

"Oh, well," said Banford, "we don't mind, do we, Nellie?"

"No," said March, "we don't mind."

The youth was very pleased. He had eaten and drunk his fill. Banford began to question him. His name was Henry Grenfel – no, he was not called Harry, always Henry. He continued to answer with courteous simplicity, grave and charming. March, who was not included, cast long, slow glances at him from her recess, as he sat there on the sofa, his hands clasping his knees, his face under the lamp bright and alert, turned to Banford. She became almost peaceful at last. He was identified with the fox – and he was here in full presence. She need not go after him any more. There in the shadow of her corner she gave herself up to a warm, relaxed peace, almost like sleep, accepting the spell that was on her. But she wished to remain hidden. She was only fully at peace whilst he forgot her, talking to Banford. Hidden in the shadow of the corner, she need not any more be divided in herself, trying to keep up two planes of consciousness. She could at last lapse into the odour of the fox.

For the youth, sitting before the fire in his uniform, sent a faint but distinct odour into the room, indefinable, but something like a wild creature. March no longer tried to reserve herself from it. She was still and soft in her corner, like a passive creature in its cave.

At last the talk dwindled. The youth relaxed his clasp of his knees, pulled himself together a little and looked round. Again he became aware of the silent, half-invisible woman in the corner.

"Well," he said unwillingly, "I suppose I'd better be going, or they'll be in bed at the Swan."

"I'm afraid they're in bed anyhow," said Banford. "They've all got this influenza."

"Have they!" he exclaimed. And he pondered. "Well," he continued, "I shall find a place somewhere."

"I'd say you could stay here, only..." Banford began.

He turned and watched her, holding his head forwards.

"What?..." he asked.

"Oh, well," she said, "propriety, I suppose..." She was rather confused.

"It wouldn't be improper, would it?" he said, gently surprised.

"Not as far as we're concerned," said Banford.

"And not as far as *I'm* concerned," he said, with grave naivety. "After all, it's my own home in a way."

Banford smiled at this.

"It's what the village will have to say," she said.

There was a moment's blank pause.

"What do you say, Nellie?" asked Banford.

"I don't mind," said March, in her distinct tone. "The village doesn't matter to me, anyhow."

"No," said the youth, quick and soft. "Why should it? I mean, what should they say?"

"Oh, well," came March's plangent, laconic voice, "they'll easily find something to say. But it makes no difference what they say. We can look after ourselves."

"Of course you can," said the youth.

"Well, then, stop if you like," said Banford. "The spare room is quite ready."

His face shone with pleasure.

"If you're quite sure it isn't troubling you too much," he said, with that soft courtesy which distinguished him.

"Oh, it's no trouble," they both said.

He looked, smiling with delight, from one to another.

"It's awfully nice not to have to turn out again, isn't it?" he said gratefully.

"I suppose it is," said Banford.

March disappeared to attend the room. Banford was as pleased and thoughtful as if she had her own brother home from France. It gave her just the same kind of gratification to attend on him, to get out the bath for him, and everything. Her natural warmth and kindliness had now an outlet. And the youth luxuriated in her sisterly attention. But it puzzled him slightly to know that March was silently working for him too. She was so curiously silent and obliterated. It seemed to him he had not really seen her. He felt he should not know her if he met her in the road.

That night March dreamt vividly. She dreamt she heard a singing outside, which she could not understand, a singing that roamed round the house, in the fields and in the darkness. It moved her so, that she felt she must weep. She went out, and suddenly she knew it was the fox singing. He was very yellow and bright, like corn. She went nearer to him, but he ran away and ceased singing. He seemed near, and she wanted to touch him. She stretched out her hand, but suddenly he bit her wrist, and at the same instant as she drew back, the fox, turning round to bound away, whisked his brush across her face, and it seemed his brush was on fire, for it seared and burned her mouth with a great pain. She awoke with the pain of it, and lay trembling as if she were really seared.

In the morning, however, she only remembered it as a distant memory. She arose and was busy preparing the house and attending to the fowls. Banford flew into the village on her bicycle to try and buy food. She was a hospitable soul. But alas, in the year 1918 there was not much food to buy. The youth came downstairs in his shirtsleeves. He was young and fresh, but he walked with his head thrust forwards so that his shoulders seemed raised and rounded, as if he had a slight curvature of the spine. It must have been only a manner of bearing himself, for he was young and vigorous. He washed himself and went outside whilst the women were preparing breakfast.

He saw everything, and examined everything. His curiosity was quick and insatiable. He compared the state of things with that which he remembered before, and cast over in his mind the effect of the changes. He watched the fowls and the ducks, to see their condition, he noticed the flight of wood pigeons overhead – they were very numerous; he saw the few apples high up, which March had not been able to reach; he remarked that they had borrowed a draw pump, presumably to empty the big soft-water cistern which was on the north side of the house.

"It's a funny, dilapidated old place," he said to the girls, as he sat at breakfast.

His eyes were wise and childish, with thinking about things. He did not say much, but ate largely. March kept her face averted. She, too, in the early morning, could not be aware of him, though something about the glint of his khaki reminded her of the brilliance of her dream fox.

During the day the girls went about their business. In the morning he attended to the guns, shot a rabbit and a wild duck that was flying high towards the wood. That was a great addition to the empty larder. The girls felt that already he had earned his keep. He said nothing about leaving, however. In the afternoon he went to the village. He came back at teatime. He had the same alert, forward-reaching look on his roundish face. He hung his hat on a peg with a little swinging gesture. He was thinking about something.

"Well," he said to the girls, as he sat at table. "What am I going to do?"

"How do you mean – what are you going to do?" said Banford.

"Where am I going to find a place in the village to stay?" he said.

"I don't know," said Banford. "Where do you think of staying?"

"Well…" he hesitated, "at the Swan they've got this flu, and at the Plough and Harrow they've got the soldiers who are collecting the hay for the army – besides, in the private houses, there's ten men and a corporal altogether billeted in the village, they tell me. I'm not sure where I could get a bed."

He left the matter to them. He was rather calm about it. March sat with her elbows on the table, her two hands supporting her chin, looking at him unconsciously. Suddenly he lifted his clouded blue eyes, and unthinkingly looked straight into March's eyes. He was startled as well as she. He too recoiled a little. March felt the same sly, taunting, knowing spark leap out of his eyes, as he turned his head aside, and fall into her soul, as it had fallen from the dark eyes of the fox. She pursed her mouth as if in pain – as if asleep too.

"Well, I don't know…" Banford was saying. She seemed reluctant, as if she were afraid of being imposed upon. She looked at March. But with her weak, troubled sight, she only saw the usual semi-abstraction on her friend's face. "Why don't you speak, Nellie?" she said.

But March was wide-eyed and silent, and the youth, as if fascinated, was watching her without moving his eyes.

"Go on – answer something," said Banford. And March turned her head slightly aside, as if coming to consciousness, or trying to come to consciousness.

"What do you expect me to say?" she asked automatically.

"Say what you think," said Banford.

"It's all the same to me," said March.

And again there was silence. A pointed light seemed to be on the boy's eyes, penetrating like a needle.

"So it is to me," said Banford. "You can stop on here if you like."

A smile like a cunning little flame came over his face suddenly and involuntarily. He dropped his head quickly to hide it, and remained with his head dropped, his face hidden.

"You can stop on here if you like. You can please yourself, Henry," Banford concluded.

Still he did not reply, but remained with his head dropped. Then he lifted his face. It was bright with a curious light, as if exultant, and his eyes were strangely clear as he watched March. She turned her face aside, her mouth suffering as if wounded, and her consciousness dim.

Banford became a little puzzled. She watched the steady, pellucid gaze of the youth's eyes as he looked at March, with the invisible smile gleaming on his face. She did not know how he was smiling, for no feature moved. It seemed only in the gleam, almost the glitter of the fine hairs on his cheeks. Then he looked, with quite a changed look, at Banford.

"I'm sure," he said in his soft, courteous voice, "you're awfully good. You're too good. You don't want to be bothered with me, I'm sure."

"Cut a bit of bread, Nellie," said Banford uneasily – adding: "It's no bother, if you like to stay. It's like having my own brother here for a few days. He's a boy like you are."

"That's awfully kind of you," the lad repeated. "I should like to stay ever so much, if you're sure I'm not a trouble to you."

"No, of course you're no trouble. I tell you, it's a pleasure to have somebody in the house beside ourselves," said warm-hearted Banford.

"But Miss March?" he said in his soft voice, looking at her.

"Oh, it's quite all right as far as I'm concerned," said March vaguely.

His face beamed, and he almost rubbed his hands with pleasure.

"Well then," he said, "I should love it, if you'd let me pay my board and help with the work."

"You've no need to talk about board," said Banford.

One or two days went by, and the youth stayed on at the farm. Banford was quite charmed by him. He was so soft and courteous in speech, not wanting to say much himself, preferring to hear what she had to say, and to laugh in his quick, half-mocking way. He helped readily with the work – but not too much. He loved to be out alone with the gun in his hands, to watch, to see. For his sharp-eyed, impersonal curiosity was insatiable, and he was most free when he was quite alone, half hidden, watching.

Particularly he watched March. She was a strange character to him. Her figure, like a graceful young man's, piqued him. Her dark eyes made something rise in his soul, with a curious elate excitement when he looked into them – an excitement he was afraid to let be seen, it was so keen and secret. And then her odd, shrewd speech made him laugh outright. He felt he must go further, he was inevitably impelled. But he put away the thought of her, and went off towards the wood's edge with the gun.

The dusk was falling as he came home, and with the dusk, a fine, late November rain. He saw the firelight leaping in the window of the sitting room, a leaping light in the little cluster of the dark buildings. And he thought to himself, it would be a good thing to have this place for his own. And then the thought entered him shrewdly – why not marry March? He stood still in the middle of the field for some moments, the dead rabbit hanging still in his hand, arrested by this thought. His mind waited in amazement – it seemed to calculate – and then he smiled curiously to himself in acquiescence. Why not? Why not, indeed? It was a good idea. What if it was rather ridiculous? What did it matter? What if she was older than he? It didn't matter. When he thought of her dark, startled, vulnerable eyes he smiled subtly to himself. He was older than she, really. He was master of her.

He scarcely admitted his intention even to himself. He kept it as a secret even from himself. It was all too uncertain as yet. He would have to see how things went. Yes, he would have to see how things went. If he wasn't careful, she would just simply mock at the idea. He knew, sly and subtle as he was, that if he went to her plainly and said: "Miss March, I love you and want you to marry me," her inevitable answer would be: "Get out. I don't want any of that tomfoolery." This was her attitude to men and their "tomfoolery". If he was not careful, she would turn round on him with her savage, sardonic ridicule, and dismiss him from the farm and from her own mind for ever. He would have to go gently. He would have to catch her as you catch a deer or a woodcock when you go out shooting. It's no good walking out into the forest and saying to the deer: "Please fall to my gun." No, it is a slow, subtle battle. When you really go out to get a deer, you gather yourself together, you coil yourself inside yourself and you advance secretly, before dawn, into the mountains. It is not so much what you do, when you go out hunting, as how you feel. You have to be subtle and cunning and absolutely fatally ready. It becomes like a fate. Your own fate overtakes and determines the fate of the deer you are hunting. First of all, even before you come in sight of your quarry, there is a strange battle, like mesmerism. Your own soul, as a hunter, has gone out to fasten on the soul of the deer, even before you see any deer. And the soul of the deer fights to escape. Even before the deer has any wind of you, it is so. It is a subtle, profound battle of wills, which takes place in the invisible. And it is a battle never finished till your bullet goes home. When you are *really* worked up to the true pitch, and you come at last into range, you don't then aim as you do when you are firing at a bottle. It is your own *will* which carries the bullet into the heart of your quarry. The bullet's flight home is a sheer projection of your own fate into the fate of the deer. It happens like a supreme wish, a supreme act of volition, not as a dodge of cleverness.

He was a huntsman in spirit, not a farmer, and not a soldier stuck in a regiment. And it was as a young hunter that he wanted to bring down March as his quarry, to make her his wife. So he gathered himself subtly together, seemed to withdraw into a kind of invisibility. He was not quite sure how he would go on. And March was suspicious as a hare. So he remained in appearance just the nice, odd stranger-youth, staying for a fortnight on the place.

He had been sawing logs for the fire in the afternoon. Darkness came very early. It was still a cold, raw mist. It was getting almost too dark to see. A pile of short sawed logs lay beside the trestle. March came to carry them indoors, or into the shed, as he was busy sawing the last log. He was working in his shirtsleeves, and did not notice her approach. She came unwillingly, as if shy. He saw her stooping to the bright-ended logs, and he stopped sawing. A fire like lightning flew down his legs in the nerves.

"March?" he said, in his quiet young voice.

She looked up from the logs she was piling.

"Yes!" she said.

He looked down on her in the dusk. He could see her not too distinctly.

"I wanted to ask you something," he said.

"Did you? What was it?" she said. Already the fright was in her voice. But she was too much mistress of herself.

"Why…" his voice seemed to draw out soft and subtle, it penetrated her nerves. "Why, what do you think it is?"

She stood up, placed her hands on her hips, and stood looking at him, transfixed, without answering. Again he burned with a sudden power.

"Well," he said, and his voice was so soft it seemed rather like a subtle touch, like the merest touch of a cat's paw, a feeling rather than a sound. "Well – I wanted to ask you to marry me."

March felt rather than heard him. She was trying in vain to turn aside her face. A great relaxation seemed to have come over her. She stood silent, her head slightly on one side. He seemed to be bending towards her, invisibly smiling. It seemed to her fine sparks came out of him.

Then very suddenly she said, "Don't try any of your tomfoolery on me."

A quiver went over his nerves. He had missed. He waited a moment to collect himself again. Then he said, putting all the strange softness into his voice, as if he were imperceptibly stroking her:

"Why, it's not tomfoolery. It's not tomfoolery. I mean it. I mean it. What makes you disbelieve me?"

He sounded hurt. And his voice had such a curious power over her, making her feel loose and relaxed. She struggled somewhere for her own power. She felt for a moment that she was lost – lost – lost. The word seemed to rock in her as if she were dying. Suddenly again she spoke.

"You don't know what you are talking about," she said, in a brief and transient stroke of scorn. "What nonsense! I'm old enough to be your mother."

"Yes, I do know what I'm talking about. Yes, I do," he persisted softly, as if he were producing his voice in her blood. "I know quite well what I'm talking about. You're not old enough to be my mother. That isn't true. And what does it matter even if it was. You can marry me whatever age we are. What is age to me? And what is age to you! Age is nothing."

A swoon went over her as he concluded. He spoke rapidly – in the rapid Cornish fashion – and his voice seemed to sound in her somewhere where she was helpless against it. "Age is nothing!" The soft, heavy insistence of it made her sway dimly out there in the darkness. She could not answer.

A great exultance leapt like fire over his limbs. He felt he had won.

"I want to marry you, you see. Why shouldn't I?" he proceeded, soft and rapid. He waited for her to answer. In the dusk he saw her almost phosphorescent. Her eyelids were dropped, her face half averted and unconscious. She seemed to be in his power. But he waited, watchful. He dared not yet touch her.

"Say then," he said. "Say then you'll marry me. Say... say!" He was softly insistent.

"What?" she asked, faint, from a distance, like one in pain. His voice was now unthinkably near and soft. He drew very near to her.

"Say yes."

"Oh, I can't," she wailed helplessly, half articulate, as if semi-conscious, and as if in pain, like one who dies. "How can I?"

"You can," he said softly, laying his head gently on her shoulder as she stood with her head averted and dropped, dazed. "You can. Yes, you can. What makes you say you can't? You can. You can." And with awful softness he bent forwards and just touched her neck with his mouth and his chin.

"Don't!" she cried, with a faint mad cry like hysteria, starting away and facing round on him. "What do you mean?" But she had no breath to speak with. It was as if she was killed.

"I mean what I say," he persisted softly and cruelly. "I want you to marry me. I want you to marry me. You know that now, don't you? You know that now? Don't you? Don't you?"

"What?" she said.

"Know," he replied.

"Yes," she said. "I know you say so."

"And you know I mean it, don't you?"

"I know you say so."

"You believe me?" he said.

She was silent for some time. Then she pursed her lips.

"I don't know what I believe," she said.

"Are you out there?" came Banford's voice, calling from the house.

"Yes, we're bringing in the logs," he answered.

"I thought you'd gone lost," said Banford disconsolately. "Hurry up, do, and come and let's have tea. The kettle's boiling."

He stooped at once to take an armful of little logs and carry them into the kitchen, where they were piled in a corner. March also helped, filling her arms and carrying the logs on her breast as if they were some heavy child. The night had fallen cold.

When the logs were all in, the two cleaned their boots noisily on the scraper outside, then rubbed them on the mat. March shut the door and took off her old felt hat – her farm-girl hat. Her thick, crisp black hair was loose, her face was pale and strained. She pushed back her hair vaguely and washed her hands. Banford came hurrying into the dimly lit kitchen to take from the oven the scones she was keeping hot.

"Whatever have you been doing all this time?" she asked fretfully. "I thought you were never coming in. And it's ages since you stopped sawing. What were you doing out there?"

"Well," said Henry, "we had to stop that hole in the barn, to keeps the rats out."

"Why, I could see you standing there in the shed. I could see your shirtsleeves," challenged Banford.

"Yes, I was just putting the saw away."

They went in to tea. March was quite mute. Her face was pale and strained and vague. The youth, who always had the same ruddy, self-contained look on his face, as though he were keeping himself to himself, had come to tea in his shirtsleeves as if he were at home. He bent over his plate as he ate his food.

"Aren't you cold?" said Banford spitefully. "In your shirtsleeves?"

He looked up at her, with his chin near his plate, and his eyes very clear, pellucid and unwavering as he watched her.

"No, I'm not cold," he said, with his usual soft courtesy. "It's much warmer in here than it is outside, you see."

"I hope it is," said Banford, feeling nettled by him. He had a strange, suave assurance, and a wide-eyed bright look that got on her nerves this evening.

"But perhaps," he said softly and courteously, "you don't like me coming to tea without my coat. I forgot that."

"Oh, I don't mind," said Banford – although she *did*.

"I'll go and get it, shall I?" he said.

March's eyes turned slowly down to him.

"No, don't you bother," she said, in her queer, twanging tone. "If you feel all right as you are, stop as you are." She spoke with a crude authority.

"Yes," said he, "I *feel* all right, if I'm not rude."

"It's usually considered rude," said Banford. "But we don't mind."

"Go along – 'considered rude'," ejaculated March. "Who considers it rude?"

"Why you do, Nellie, in anybody else," said Banford, bridling a little behind her spectacles, and feeling her food stick in her throat.

But March had again gone vague and unheeding, chewing her food as if she did not know she was eating at all. And the youth looked from one to another, with bright, watchful eyes.

Banford was offended. For all his suave courtesy and soft voice, the youth seemed to her impudent. She did not like to look at him. She did not like to meet his clear, watchful eyes; she did not like to see the strange glow in his face, his cheeks with their delicate fine hair, and his ruddy skin that was quite dull and yet which seemed to burn with a curious heat of life. It made her feel a little ill to look at him – the quality of his physical presence was too penetrating, too hot.

After tea, the evening was very quiet. The youth rarely went into the village. As a rule he read – he was a great reader, in his own hours. That is, when he did begin, he read absorbedly. But he was not very eager to begin. Often he walked about the fields and along the hedges alone in the dark at night, prowling with a queer instinct for the night, and listening to the wild sounds.

Tonight, however, he took a Captain Mayne Reid book from Banford's shelf and sat down with knees wide apart and immersed himself in his story. His brownish fair hair was long, and lay on his head like a thick cap, combed sideways. He was still in his shirtsleeves and, bending forwards under the lamplight, with his knees stuck wide apart and the book in his hand, and his whole figure absorbed in the rather strenuous business of reading, he gave Banford's sitting room the look of a lumber camp. She resented this. For on her sitting-room floor she had a red Turkey rug and dark stain round, the fireplace had fashionable green tiles, the piano stood open with the latest dance music – she played quite well – and on the walls were March's hand-painted swans and water lilies. Moreover, with the logs nicely, tremulously burning in the grate, the thick curtains drawn, the doors all shut and the pine trees hissing and shuddering in the wind outside, it was cosy, it was refined and nice. She resented the big, raw, long-legged youth sticking his khaki knees out and sitting there with his soldier's shirt cuffs buttoned on his thick red wrists. From time to time he turned a page, and from time to time he gave a sharp look at the fire, settling the logs. Then he immersed himself again in the intense and isolated business of reading.

March, on the far side of the table, was spasmodically crocheting. Her mouth was pursed in an odd way, as when she had dreamt the fox's brush burned it, her beautiful, crisp black hair strayed in wisps. But her whole figure was absorbed in its bearing, as if she herself was miles away. In a sort of semi-dream she seemed to be hearing the fox singing round the house in the wind – singing wildly and sweetly and like a madness. With red but well-shaped hands she slowly crocheted the white cotton, very slowly, awkwardly.

Banford was also trying to read, sitting in her low chair. But between those two she felt fidgety. She kept moving and looking round and listening to the wind, and glancing secretly from one to the other of her companions. March, seated on a straight chair, with her knees in their close breeches crossed, and slowly, laboriously crocheting, was also a trial.

"Oh dear!" said Banford. "My eyes are bad tonight." And she pressed her fingers on her eyes.

The youth looked up at her with his clear bright look, but did not speak.

"Are they, Jill?" said March absently.

Then the youth began to read again, and Banford perforce returned to her book. But she could not keep still. After a while she looked up at March, and a queer, almost malignant little smile was on her thin face.

"A penny for them, Nell," she said suddenly.

March looked round with big, startled black eyes, and went pale as if with terror. She had been listening to the fox singing so tenderly, so tenderly, as he wandered round the house.

"What?" she said vaguely.

"A penny for them," said Banford sarcastically. "Or twopence, if they're as deep as all that."

The youth was watching with bright clear eyes from beneath the lamp.

"Why," came March's vague voice, "what do you want to waste your money for?"

"I thought it would be well spent," said Banford.

"I wasn't thinking of anything except the way the wind was blowing," said March.

"Oh dear," replied Banford, "I could have had as original thoughts as that myself. I'm afraid I *have* wasted my money this time."

"Well, you needn't pay," said March.

The youth suddenly laughed. Both women looked at him, March rather surprised-looking, as if she had hardly known he was there.

"Why, do you ever pay up on these occasions?" he asked.

"Oh yes," said Banford. "We always do. I've sometimes had to pass a shilling a week to Nellie in the wintertime. It costs much less in summer."

"What, paying for each other's thoughts?" he laughed.

"Yes, when we've absolutely come to the end of everything else."

He laughed quickly, wrinkling his nose sharply like a puppy and laughing with quick pleasure, his eyes shining.

"It's the first time I ever heard of that," he said.

"I guess you'd hear of it often enough if you stayed a winter on Bailey Farm," said Banford lamentably.

"Do you get so tired, then?" he asked.

"So bored," said Banford.

"Oh!" he said gravely. "But why should you be bored?"

"Who wouldn't be bored?" said Banford.

"I'm sorry to hear that," he said gravely.

"You must be, if you were hoping to have a lively time here," said Banford.

He looked at her long and gravely.

"Well," he said, with his odd young seriousness, "it's quite lively enough for me."

"I'm glad to hear it," said Banford.

And she returned to her book. In her thin, frail hair were already many threads of grey, though she was not yet thirty. The boy did not look down, but turned his eyes to March, who was sitting with pursed mouth laboriously crocheting, her eyes wide and absent. She had a warm, pale, fine skin, and a delicate nose. Her pursed mouth looked shrewish. But the shrewish look was contradicted by the curious lifted arch of her dark brows, and the wideness of her eyes; a look of startled wonder and vagueness. She was listening again for the fox who seemed to have wandered further off into the night.

From under the edge of the lamplight the boy sat with his face looking up, watching her silently, his eyes round and very clear and intent. Banford, biting her fingers irritably, was glancing at him under her hair. He sat there perfectly still, his ruddy face tilted up from the low level under the light, on the edge of the dimness, and watching with perfect abstract intentness. March suddenly lifted her great dark eyes from her crocheting, and saw him. She started, giving a little exclamation.

"There he *is*!" she cried involuntarily, as if terribly startled.

Banford looked around in amazement, sitting up straight.

"Whatever has got you, Nellie?" she cried.

But March, her face flushed a delicate rose colour, was looking away to the door.

"Nothing! Nothing!" she said crossly. "Can't one speak?"

"Yes, if you speak sensibly," said Banford. "Whatever did you mean?"

"I don't know what I meant," cried March testily.

"Oh, Nellie, I hope you aren't going jumpy and nervy. I feel I can't stand another *thing*! Whoever did you mean? Did you mean Henry?" cried poor frightened Banford.

"Yes, I suppose so," said March laconically. She would never confess to the fox.

"Oh dear, my nerves are all gone for tonight," wailed Banford.

At nine o'clock March brought in a tray with bread and cheese and tea – Henry had confessed that he liked a cup of tea. Banford drank a glass of milk and ate a little bread. And soon she said:

"I'm going to bed, Nellie. I'm all nerves tonight. Are you coming?"

"Yes, I'm coming the minute I've taken the tray away," said March.

"Don't be long then," said Banford fretfully. "Goodnight, Henry. You'll see the fire is safe, if you come up last, won't you?"

"Yes, Miss Banford, I'll see it's safe," he replied, in his reassuring way.

March was lighting the candle to go to the kitchen. Banford took her candle and went upstairs. When March came back to the fire she said to him:

"I suppose we can trust you to put out the fire and everything?"

She stood there with her hand on her hip, and one knee loose, her head averted shyly, as if she could not look at him. He had his face lifted, watching her.

"Come and sit down a minute," he said softly.

"No, I'll be going. Jill will be waiting, and she'll get upset if I don't come."

"What made you jump like that this evening?" he asked.

"When did I jump?" she retorted, looking at him.

"Why, just now you did," he said. "When you cried out."

"Oh!" she said. "Then! Why, I thought you were the fox!" And her face screwed into a queer smile, half ironic.

"The fox! Why the fox?" he asked softly.

"Why, one evening last summer when I was out with the gun, I saw the fox in the grass nearly at my feet, looking straight up at me. I don't know – I suppose he made an impression on me." She turned aside her head again, and let one foot stray loose, self-consciously.

"And did you shoot him?" asked the boy.

"No, he gave me such a start, staring straight at me as he did, and then stopping to look back at me over his shoulder with a laugh on his face."

"A laugh on his face!" repeated Henry, also laughing. "He frightened you, did he?"

"No, he didn't frighten me. He made an impression on me, that's all."

"And you thought I was the fox, did you?" he laughed, with the same queer, quick little laugh, like a puppy wrinkling its nose.

"Yes, I did, for the moment," she said. "Perhaps he'd been in my mind without my knowing."

"Perhaps you think I've come to steal your chickens or something," he said, with the same young laugh.

But she only looked at him with a wide, dark, vacant eye.

"It's the first time," he said, "that I've ever been taken for a fox. Won't you sit down for a minute?" His voice was very soft and cajoling.

"No," she said. "Jill will be waiting." But still she did not go, but stood with one foot loose and her face turned aside, just outside the circle of light.

"But won't you answer my question?" he said, lowering his voice still more.

"I don't know what question you mean."

"Yes, you do. Of course you do. I mean the question of you marrying me."

"No, I shan't answer that question," she said flatly.

"Won't you?" The queer young laugh came on his nose again. "Is it because I'm like the fox? Is that why?" And still he laughed.

She turned and looked at him with a long, slow look.

"I wouldn't let that put you against me," he said. "Let me turn the lamp low, and come and sit down a minute."

He put his red hand under the glow of the lamp, and suddenly made the light very dim. March stood there in the dimness quite shadowy, but unmoving. He rose silently to his feet, on his long legs. And now his voice was extraordinarily soft and suggestive, hardly audible.

"You'll stay a moment," he said. "Just a moment." And he put his hand on her shoulder. She turned her face from him. "I'm sure you don't really think I'm the fox," he said, with the same softness and with a suggestion of laughter in his tone, a subtle mockery. "Do you now?" And he drew her gently towards him and kissed her neck softly. She winced and trembled and hung away. But his strong young arm held her, and he kissed her softly again, still on the neck, for her face was averted.

"Won't you answer my question? Won't you now?" came his soft, lingering voice. He was trying to draw her near to kiss her face. And he kissed her cheek softly, near the ear.

At that moment Banford's voice was heard calling fretfully, crossly from upstairs.

"There's Jill!" cried March, starting and drawing erect.

And as she did so, quick as lightning he kissed her on the mouth, with a quick brushing kiss. It seemed to burn through her every fibre. She gave a queer little cry.

"You will, won't you? You will?" he insisted softly.

"Nellie! Nellie! Whatever are you so long for?" came Banford's faint cry from the outer darkness.

But he held her fast, and was murmuring with that intolerable softness and insistency:

"You will, won't you? Say yes! Say yes!"

March, who felt as if the fire had gone through her and scathed her, and as if she could do no more, murmured:

"Yes! Yes! Anything you like! Anything you like! Only let me go! Jill's calling."

"You know you've promised," he said insidiously.

"Yes! Yes! I do!..." Her voice suddenly rose into a shrill cry. "All right, Jill, I'm coming."

Startled, he let her go, and she went straight upstairs.

In the morning at breakfast, after he had looked round the place and attended to the stock, and thought to himself that one could live easily enough here, he said to Banford:

"Do you know what, Miss Banford?"

"Well, what?" said the good-natured, nervy Banford.

He looked at March, who was spreading jam on her bread.

"Shall I tell?" he said to her.

She looked up at him, and a deep pink colour flushed over her face.

"Yes, if you mean Jill," she said. "I hope you won't go talking all over the village, that's all." And she swallowed her dry bread with difficulty.

"Whatever's coming?" said Banford, looking up with wide, tired, slightly reddened eyes. She was a thin, frail little thing, and her hair, which was delicate and thin, was bobbed, so it hung softly by her worn face in its faded brown and grey.

"Why, what do you think?" he said, smiling like one who has a secret.

"How do I know!" said Banford.

"Can't you guess?" he said, making bright eyes, and smiling, pleased with himself.

"I'm sure I can't. What's more, I'm not going to try."

"Nellie and I are going to be married."

Banford put down her knife out of her thin, delicate fingers, as if she would never take it up to eat any more. She stared with blank, reddened eyes.

"You what?" she exclaimed.

"We're going to get married. Aren't we, Nellie?" and he turned to March.

"You say so, anyway," said March laconically. But again she flushed with an agonized flush. She, too, could swallow no more.

Banford looked at her like a bird that has been shot: a poor little sick bird. She gazed at her with all her wounded soul in her face, at the deep-flushed March.

"Never!" she exclaimed, helpless.

"It's quite right," said the bright and gloating youth.

Banford turned aside her face, as if the sight of the food on the table made her sick. She sat like this for some moments, as if she were sick. Then, with one hand on the edge of the table, she rose to her feet.

"I'll *never* believe it, Nellie," she cried. "It's absolutely impossible!"

Her plaintive, fretful voice had a thread of hot anger and despair.

"Why? Why shouldn't you believe it?" asked the youth, with all his soft, velvety impertinence in his voice.

Banford looked at him from her wide, vague eyes, as if he were some creature in a museum.

"Oh," she said languidly, "because she can never be such a fool. She can't lose her self-respect to such an extent." Her voice was cold and plaintive, drifting.

"In what way will she lose her self-respect?" asked the boy.

Banford looked at him with vague fixity from behind her spectacles.

"If she hasn't lost it already," she said.

He became very red, vermilion, under the slow vague stare from behind the spectacles.

"I don't see it at all," he said.

"Probably you don't. I shouldn't expect you would," said Banford, with that straying mild tone of remoteness which made her words even more insulting.

He sat stiff in his chair, staring with hot blue eyes from his scarlet face. An ugly look had come on his brow.

"My word, she doesn't know what she's letting herself in for," said Banford, in her plaintive, drifting, insulting voice.

"What has it got to do with you, anyway?" said the youth in a temper.

"More than it has to do with you, probably," she replied, plaintive and venomous.

"Oh, has it! I don't see that at all," he jerked out.

"No, you wouldn't," she answered, drifting.

"Anyhow," said March, pushing back her hair and rising uncouthly, "it's no good arguing about it." And she seized the bread and the teapot, and strode away to the kitchen.

Banford let her fingers stray across her brow and along her hair, like one bemused. Then she turned and went away upstairs.

Henry sat stiff and sulky in his chair, with his face and his eyes on fire. March came and went, clearing the table. But Henry sat on, stiff with temper. He took no notice of her. She had regained her composure and her soft, even, creamy complexion. But her mouth was pursed up. She glanced at him each time as she came to take things from the table, glanced from her large, curious eyes, more in curiosity than anything. Such a long, red-faced sulky boy! That was all he was. He seemed as remote from her as if his red face were a red chimney pot on a cottage across the fields, and she looked at him just as objectively, as remotely.

At length he got up and stalked out into the fields with the gun. He came in only at dinner time, with the Devil still in his face, but his manners quite polite. Nobody said anything particular, they sat each one at the sharp corner of a triangle, in obstinate remoteness. In the afternoon he went out again at once with the gun. He came in at nightfall with a rabbit and a pigeon. He stayed in all evening, but hardly opened his mouth. He was in the devil of a temper, feeling he had been insulted.

Banford's eyes were red, she had evidently been crying. But her manner was more remote and supercilious than ever, the way she turned her head if he spoke at all, as if he were some tramp or inferior intruder of that sort, made his blue eyes go almost black with rage. His face looked sulkier. But he never forgot his polite intonation, if he opened his mouth to speak.

March seemed to flourish in this atmosphere. She seemed to sit between the two antagonists with a little wicked smile on her face, enjoying herself. There was even a sort of complacency in the way she laboriously crocheted, this evening.

When he was in bed, the youth could hear the two women talking and arguing in their room. He sat up in bed and strained his ears to hear what they said. But he could hear nothing, it was too far off. Yet he could hear the soft, plaintive drip of Banford's voice, and March's deeper note.

The night was quiet, frosty. Big stars were snapping outside, beyond the ridge-tops of the pine trees. He listened and listened. In the distance he heard a fox yelping, and the dogs from the farms barking in answer. But it was not that he wanted to hear. It was what the two women were saying.

He got stealthily out of bed and stood by his door. He could hear no more than before. Very, very carefully he began to lift the door latch. After quite a time he had his door open. Then he stepped stealthily out into the passage. The old oak planks were cold under his feet, and they creaked preposterously. He crept very, very gently up the one step, and along by the wall, till he stood outside their door. And there he held his breath and listened. Banford's voice:

"No, I simply couldn't stand it. I should be dead in a month. Which is just what he would be aiming at, of course. That would just be his game, to see me in the churchyard. No, Nellie, if you were to do such a thing as marry him, you could never stop here. I couldn't, I couldn't live in the same house with him. Oh!... I feel quite sick with the smell of his clothes. And his red face simply turns me over. I can't eat my food when he's at the table. What a fool I was ever to let him stop. One ought *never* to try to do a kind action. It always flies back in your face like a boomerang."

"Well, he's only got two more days," said March.

"Yes, thank Heaven. And when he's gone he'll never come in this house again. I feel so bad while he's here. And I know, I know he's only counting what he can get out of you. I *know* that's all it is. He's just a good-for-nothing, who doesn't want to work, and who thinks he'll live on us. But he won't live on me. If you're such a fool, then it's your own lookout. Mrs Burgess knew him all the time he was here. And the old man could never get him to do any steady work. He was off with the gun on every occasion, just as he is now. Nothing but the gun! Oh, I do hate it. You don't know what you're doing, Nellie, you don't. If you marry him, he'll just make a fool of you. He'll go off and leave you stranded. I know he will, if he can't get Bailey Farm out of us – and he's not going to, while I live. While I live he's never going to set foot here. I know what it would be. He'd soon think he was master of both of us, and he thinks he's master of you already."

"But he isn't," said Nellie.

"He thinks he is, anyway. And that's what he wants: to come and be master here. Yes, imagine it! That's what we've got the place together for, is it, to be bossed and bullied by a hateful red-faced boy, a beastly labourer. Oh we *did* make a mistake when we let him stop. We ought never to have lowered ourselves. And I've had such a fight with all the people here not to be pulled down to their level. No, he's not coming here. And then you see – if he can't have the place, he'll run off to Canada or somewhere again, as if he'd never known you. And here you'll be, absolutely ruined and made a fool of. I know I shall never have any peace of mind again."

"We'll tell him he can't come here. We'll tell him that," said March.

"Oh, don't you bother, I'm going to tell him that, and other things as well, before he goes. He's not going to have all his own way while I've got the strength left to speak. Oh, Nellie, he'll despise you, he'll despise you like the awful beast he is, if you give way to him. I'd no more trust him than I'd trust a cat not to steal. He's deep, he's deep, and he's bossy, and he's selfish through and through, as cold as ice. All he wants is to make use of you. And when you're no more use to him, then I pity you."

"I don't think he's as bad as all that," said March.

"No, because he's been playing up to you. But you'll find out, if you see much more of him. Oh, Nellie, I can't bear to think of it."

"Well, it won't hurt you, Jill darling."

"Won't it! Won't it! I shall never know a moment's peace again while I live, nor a moment's happiness. No, Nellie…" and Banford began to weep bitterly.

The boy outside could hear the stifled sound of the woman's sobbing, and could hear March's soft, deep, tender voice comforting, with wonderful gentleness and tenderness, the weeping woman.

His eyes were so round and wide that he seemed to see the whole night, and his ears were almost jumping off his head. He was frozen stiff. He crept back to bed, but felt as if the top of his head were coming off. He could not sleep. He could not keep still. He rose, quietly dressed himself, and crept out onto the landing once more. The women were silent. He went softly downstairs and out to the kitchen.

Then he put on his boots and overcoat, and took the gun. He did not think to go away from the farm. No, he only took the gun. As softly as possible he unfastened the door and went out into the frosty December night. The air was still, the stars bright, the pine trees seemed to bristle audibly in the sky. He went stealthily away down a fence side, looking for something to shoot. At the same time he remembered that he ought not to shoot and frighten the women.

So he prowled round the edge of the gorse cover, and through the grove of tall old hollies to the woodside. There he skirted the fence, peering through the darkness with dilated eyes that seemed to be able to grow black and full of sight in the dark, like a cat's. An owl was slowly and mournfully whooing round a great oak tree. He stepped stealthily with his gun, listening, listening, watching.

As he stood under the oaks of the wood edge he heard the dogs from the neighbouring cottage, up the hill, yelling suddenly and startlingly, and the wakened dogs from the farms around barking answer. And suddenly it seemed to him England was little and tight, he felt the landscape was constricted even in the dark, and that there were too many dogs in the night, making a noise like a fence of sound, like the network of English hedges netting the view. He felt the fox didn't have a chance. For it must be the fox that had started all this hullabaloo.

Why not watch for him, anyhow! He would no doubt be coming sniffing round. The lad walked downhill to where the farmstead with its few pine trees crouched blackly. In the angle of the long shed, in the black dark, he crouched down. He knew the fox would be coming. It seemed to him it would be the last of the foxes in this loudly barking, thick-voiced England, tight with innumerable little houses.

He sat a long time with his eyes fixed unchanging upon the open gateway, where a little light seemed to fall from the stars or from the horizon, who knows. He was sitting on a log in a dark corner with the gun across his knees. The pine trees snapped. Once a chicken fell off its perch in the barn, with a loud crawk and cackle and commotion that startled him, and he stood up, watching with all his eyes, thinking it might be a rat. But he felt it was nothing. So he sat down again with the gun on his knees and his hands tucked in to keep them warm, and his eyes fixed unblinking on the pale reach of the open gateway. He felt he could smell the hot, sickly, rich smell of live chickens on the cold air.

And then – a shadow. A sliding shadow in the gateway. He gathered all his vision into a concentrated spark, and saw the shadow of the fox, the fox creeping on his belly through the gate. There he went, on his belly like a snake. The boy smiled to himself and brought the gun to his shoulder. He knew quite well what would happen. He knew the fox would go to where the fowl door was boarded up, and sniff there. He knew he would lie there for a minute, sniffing the fowls within. And then he would start again prowling under the edge of the old barn, waiting to get in.

The fowl door was at the top of a slight incline. Soft, soft as a shadow the fox slid up this incline, and crouched with his nose to the boards. And at the same moment there was an awful crash of a gun reverberating between the old buildings, as if all the night had gone smash. But the boy watched keenly. He saw even the white belly of the fox as the beast beat his paws in death. So he went forwards.

There was a commotion everywhere. The fowls were scuffling and crawking, the ducks were quark-quarking, the pony had stamped wildly to his feet. But the fox was on his side, struggling in his last tremors. The boy bent over him and smelt his foxy smell.

There was a sound of a window opening upstairs, then March's voice calling:

"Who is it?"

"It's me," said Henry. "I've shot the fox."

"Oh, goodness! You nearly frightened us to death."

"Did I? I'm awfully sorry."

"Whatever made you get up?"

"I heard him about."

"And have you shot him?"

"Yes, he's here," and the boy stood in the yard holding up the warm, dead brute. "You can't see, can you? Wait a minute." And he took his flashlight from his pocket, and flashed it onto the dead animal. He was holding it by the brush. March saw, in the middle of the darkness, just the reddish fleece and the white belly and the white underneath of the pointed chin, and the queer, dangling paws. She did not know what to say.

"He's a beauty," he said. "He will make you a lovely fur."

"You don't catch me wearing a fox fur," she replied.

"Oh!" he said. And he switched off the light.

"Well I should think you'll come in and go to bed again now," she said.

"Probably I shall. What time is it?"

"What time is it, Jill?" called March's voice. It was a quarter to one.

That night March had another dream. She dreamt that Banford was dead, and that she, March, was sobbing her heart out. Then she had to put Banford into her coffin. And the coffin was the rough wood box in which the bits of chopped wood were kept in the kitchen, by the fire. This was the coffin, and there was no other, and March was in agony and dazed bewilderment, looking for something to line the box with, something to make it soft with, something to cover up the poor dead darling. Because she couldn't lay her in there just in her white thin nightdress, in the horrible wood box. So she hunted and hunted, and picked up thing after thing, and threw it aside in the agony of dream frustration. And in her dream despair all she could find that would do was a fox skin. She knew that it wasn't right, that this was not what she could have. But it was all she could find. And so she folded the brush of the fox, and laid her darling Jill's head on this, and she brought round the skin of the fox and laid it on the top of the body, so that it seemed to make a whole ruddy, fiery coverlet, and she cried and cried, and woke to find the tears streaming down her face.

The first thing that both she and Banford did in the morning was to go out to see the fox. He had hung it up by the heels in the shed, with its poor brush falling backwards. It was a lovely dog fox in its prime with a handsome thick winter coat: a lovely golden-red colour, with grey as it passed to the belly, and belly all white, and a great full brush with a delicate black and grey and pure-white tip.

"Poor brute!" said Banford. "If it wasn't such a thieving wretch, you'd feel sorry for it."

March said nothing, but stood with her foot trailing aside, one hip out; her face was pale and her eyes big and black, watching the dead animal that was suspended upside down. White and soft as snow his belly; white and soft as snow. She passed her hand softly down it. And his wonderful black-glinted brush was full and frictional, wonderful. She passed her hand down this also, and quivered. Time after time she took the full fur of that thick tail between her hand and passed her hand slowly downwards. Wonderful sharp thick splendour of a tail! And he was dead! She pursed her lips, and her eyes went black and vacant. Then she took the head in her hand.

Henry was sauntering up, so Banford walked rather pointedly away. March stood there bemused, with the head of the fox in her hand. She was wondering, wondering, wondering over his long fine muzzle. For some reason it reminded her of a spoon or a spatula. She felt she could not understand it. The beast was a strange beast to her, incomprehensible, out of her range. Wonderful silver whiskers he had, like ice threads. And pricked ears with hair inside. But that long, long, slender spoon of a nose! And the marvellous white teeth beneath! It was to thrust forwards and bite with, deep, deep into the living prey, to bite and bite the blood.

"He's a beauty, isn't he?" said Henry, standing by.

"Oh yes, he's a fine big fox. I wonder how many chickens he's responsible for," she replied.

"A good many. Do you think he's the same one you saw in the summer?"

"I should think very likely he is," she replied.

He watched her, but he could make nothing of her. Partly she was so shy and virgin, and partly she was so grim, matter of fact, shrewish. What she said to him seemed so different from the look of her big, queer, dark eyes.

"Are you going to skin him?" she asked.

"Yes, when I've had breakfast, and got a board to peg him on."

"My word, what a strong smell he's got! Pooo! It'll take some washing off one's hands. I don't know why I was so silly as to handle him." And she looked at her right hand, that had passed down his belly and along his tail, and had even got a tiny streak of blood from one dark place in his fur.

"Have you seen the chickens when they smell him, how frightened they are?" he said.

"Yes, aren't they!"

"You must mind you don't get some of his fleas."

"Oh, fleas!" she replied, nonchalant.

Later in the day she saw the fox's skin nailed flat on a board, as if crucified. It gave her an uneasy feeling.

The boy was angry. He went about with his mouth shut, as if he had swallowed part of his chin. But in behaviour he was polite and affable. He did not say anything about his intention. And he left March alone.

That evening they sat in the dining room. Banford wouldn't have him in her sitting room any more. There was a very big log on the fire. And everybody was busy. Banford had letters to write, March was sewing a dress, and he was mending some little contrivance.

Banford stopped her letter-writing from time to time to look round and rest her eyes. The boy had his head down, his face hidden over his job.

"Let's see," said Banford. "What train do you go by, Henry?"

He looked up straight at her.

"The morning train. In the morning," he said.

"What, the eight-ten or the eleven-twenty?"

"The eleven-twenty, I suppose," he said.

"That is the day after tomorrow?" said Banford.

"Yes, the day after tomorrow."

"Mmm!" murmured Banford, and she returned to her writing. But as she was licking her envelope, she asked:

"And what plans have you made for the future, if I may ask?"

"Plans?" he said, his face very bright and angry.

"I mean about you and Nellie, if you are going on with this business. When do you expect the wedding to come off?" She spoke in a jeering tone.

"Oh, the wedding!" he replied. "I don't know."

"Don't you know anything?" said Banford. "Are you going to clear out on Friday and leave things no more settled than they are?"

"Well, why shouldn't I? We can always write letters."

"Yes, of course you can. But I wanted to know because of this place. If Nellie is going to get married all of a sudden, I shall have to be looking round for a new partner."

"Couldn't she stay on here if she was married?" he said. He knew quite well what was coming.

"Oh," said Banford, "this is no place for a married couple. There's not enough work to keep a man going, for one thing. And there's no money to be made. It's quite useless your thinking of staying on here if you marry. Absolutely!"

"Yes, but I wasn't thinking of staying on here," he said.

"Well, that's what I want to know. And what about Nellie, then? How long is she going to be here with me, in that case?"

The two antagonists looked at one another.

"That I can't say," he answered.

"Oh, go along," she cried petulantly. "You must have some idea what you are going to do if you ask a woman to marry you. Unless it's all a hoax."

"Why should it be a hoax? I am going back to Canada."

"And taking her with you?"

"Yes, certainly."

"You hear that, Nellie?" said Banford.

March, who had had her head bent over her sewing, now looked up with a sharp pink blush on her face and a queer, sardonic laugh in her eyes and on her twisted mouth.

"That's the first time I've heard that I was going to Canada," she said.

"Well you have to hear it for the first time, haven't you?" said the boy.

"Yes, I suppose I have," she said nonchalantly. And she went back to her sewing.

"You're quite ready, are you, to go to Canada? Are you, Nellie?" asked Banford.

March looked up again. She let her shoulders go slack, and let her hand that held the needle lie loose in her lap.

"It depends on *how* I'm going," she said. "I don't think I want to go jammed up in the steerage, as a soldier's wife. I'm afraid I'm not used to that way."

The boy watched her with bright eyes.

"Would you rather stay over here while I go first?" he asked.

"I would, if that's the only alternative," she replied.

"That's much the wisest. Don't make it any fixed engagement," said Banford. "Leave yourself free to go or not after he's got back and found you a place, Nellie. Anything else is madness, madness."

"Don't you think," said the youth, "we ought to get married before I go – and then go together, or separate, according to how it happens?"

"I think it's a *terrible* idea," cried Banford.

But the boy was watching March.

"What do you think?" he asked her.

She let her eyes stray vaguely into space.

"Well, I don't know," she said. "I shall have to think about it."

"Why?" he asked pertinently.

"Why?" She repeated his question in a mocking way, and looked at him, laughing, though her face was pink again. "I should think there's plenty of reasons why."

He watched her in silence. She seemed to have escaped him. She had got into league with Banford against him. There was again the queer sardonic look about her; she would mock stoically at everything he said or which life offered.

"Of course," he said, "I don't want to press you to do anything you don't wish to do."

"I should think not, indeed," cried Banford indignantly.

At bedtime Banford said plaintively to March:

"You take my hot bottle up for me, Nellie, will you?"

"Yes, I'll do it," said March, with the kind of willing unwillingness she so often showed towards her beloved but uncertain Jill.

The two women went upstairs. After a time March called from the top of the stairs: "Goodnight, Henry. I shan't be coming down. You'll see to the lamp and the fire, won't you?"

The next day Henry went about with the cloud on his brow and his young cub's face shut up tight. He was cogitating all the time. He had wanted March to marry him and go back to Canada with him. And he had been sure she would do it. Why he wanted her, he didn't know. But he did want her. He had set his mind on her. And he was convulsed with a youth's fury at being thwarted. To be thwarted, to be thwarted! It made him so furious inside that he did not know what to do with himself. But he kept himself in hand. Because even now things might turn out differently. She might come over to him. Of course she might. It was her business to do so.

Things drew to a tension again towards evening. He and Banford had avoided each other all day. In fact Banford went into the little town by the eleven-twenty train. It was market day. She arrived back on the four-twenty-five. Just as the night was falling, Henry saw her little figure in a dark-blue coat and a dark-blue tam-o'-shanter hat crossing the first meadow from the station. He stood under one of the wild pear trees, with the old dead leaves round his feet. And he watched the little blue figure advancing persistently over the rough winter-ragged meadow.

She had her arms full of parcels, and advanced slowly, frail thing she was, but with that devilish little certainty which he so detested in her. He stood invisible under the pear tree, watching her every step. And if looks could have affected her, she would have felt a log of iron on each of her ankles as she made her way forwards. "You're a nasty little thing, you are," he was saying softly, across the distance. "You're a nasty little thing. I hope you'll be paid back for all the harm you've done me for nothing. I hope you will – you nasty little thing. I hope you'll have to pay for it. You will, if wishes are anything. You nasty little creature that you are."

She was toiling slowly up the slope. But if she had been slipping back at every step towards the bottomless pit, he would not have gone to help her with her parcels. Aha, there went March, striding with her long land stride in her breeches and her short tunic! Striding downhill at a great pace, and even running a few steps now and then, in her great solicitude and desire to come to the rescue of the little Banford. The boy watched her with rage in his heart. See her leap a ditch, and run, run as if a house was on fire, just to get to that creeping dark little object down there! So the Banford just stood still and waited. And March strode up and took *all* the parcels except a bunch of yellow chrysanthemums. These the Banford still carried – yellow chrysanthemums!

"Yes, you look well, don't you," he said, softly into the dusk air. "You look well, pottering up there with a bunch of flowers, you do. I'd make you eat them for your tea, if you hug them so tight. And I'd give them you for breakfast again, I would. I'd give you flowers. Nothing but flowers."

He watched the progress of the two women. He could hear their voices: March always outspoken and rather scolding in her tenderness, Banford murmuring rather vaguely. They were evidently good friends. He could not hear what they said till they came to the fence of the home meadow which they must climb. Then he saw March manfully climbing over the bars with all her packages in her arms, and on the still air he heard Banford's fretful:

"Why don't you let me help you with the parcels?" She had a queer plaintive hitch in her voice. Then came March's robust and reckless:

"Oh, I can manage. Don't you bother about me. You've all you can do to get yourself over."

"Yes, that's all very well," said Banford fretfully. "You say *Don't you bother about me*, and then all the while you feel injured because nobody thinks of you."

"When do I feel injured?" said March.

"Always. You always feel injured. Now you're feeling injured because I won't have that boy to come and live on the farm."

"I'm not feeling injured at all," said March.

"I know you are. When he's gone you'll sulk over it. I know you will."

"Shall I?" said March. "We'll see."

"Yes, we *shall* see, unfortunately. I can't think how you can make yourself so cheap. I can't *imagine* how you can lower yourself like it."

"I haven't lowered myself," said March.

"I don't know what you call it, then. Letting a boy like that come so cheeky and impudent, and make a mug of you. I don't know what you think of yourself. How much respect do you think he's going to have for you afterwards? My word, I wouldn't be in your shoes if you married him."

"Of course you wouldn't. My boots are a good bit too big for you, and not half dainty enough," said March, with rather a misfire sarcasm.

"I thought you had too much pride, really I did. A woman's got to hold herself high, especially with a youth like that. Why, he's impudent. Even the way he forced himself on us at the start."

"We asked him to stay," said March.

"Not till he'd almost forced us to. And then he's so cocky and self-assured. My word, he puts my back up. I simply can't imagine how you can let him treat you so cheaply."

"I don't let him treat me cheaply," said March. "Don't you worry yourself, nobody's going to treat me cheaply. And even you aren't, either." She had a tender defiance, and a certain fire in her voice.

"Yes, it's sure to come back to me," said Banford bitterly. "That's always the end of it. I believe you only do it to spite me."

They went now in silence up the steep grassy slope and over the brow through the gorse bushes. On the other side of the hedge the boy followed in the dusk, at some little distance. Now and then, through the huge ancient hedge of hawthorn, risen into trees, he saw the two dark figures creeping up the hill. As he came to the top of the slope he saw the homestead dark in the twilight, with a huge old pear tree leaning from the near gable, and a little yellow light twinkling in the small side windows of the kitchen. He heard the clink of the latch and saw the kitchen door open into light as the two women went indoors. So they were at home.

And so! This was what they thought of him. It was rather in his nature to be a listener, so he was not at all surprised whatever he heard. The things people said about him always missed him personally. He was only rather surprised at the women's way with one another. And he disliked the Banford with an acid dislike. And he felt drawn to the March again. He felt again irresistibly drawn to her. He felt there was a secret bond, a secret thread between him and her, something very exclusive, which shut out everybody else and made him and her possess each other in secret.

He hoped again that she would have him. He hoped with his blood suddenly firing up that she would agree to marry him quite quickly: at Christmas very likely. Christmas was not far off. He wanted, whatever else happened, to snatch her into a hasty marriage and a consummation with him. Then for the future, they could arrange later. But he hoped it would happen as he wanted it. He hoped that tonight she would stay a little while with him after Banford had gone upstairs. He hoped he could touch her soft, creamy cheek, her strange, frightened face. He hoped he could look into her dilated, frightened dark eyes, quite near. He hoped he might even put his hand on her bosom and feel her soft breasts under her tunic. His heart beat deep and powerful as he thought of that. He wanted very much to do so. He wanted to make sure of her soft woman's breasts under her tunic. She always kept the brown linen coat buttoned so close up to her throat. It seemed to him like some perilous secret, that her soft woman's breasts must be buttoned up in that uniform. It seemed to him moreover that they were so much softer, tenderer, more lovely and lovable, shut up in that tunic, than were the Banford's breasts, under her soft blouses and chiffon dresses. The Banford would have little iron breasts, he said to himself. For all her frailty and fretfulness and delicacy, she would have tiny iron breasts. But March, under her crude, fast, workman's tunic, would have soft white breasts, white and unseen. So he told himself, and his blood burned.

When he went in to tea, he had a surprise. He appeared at the inner door, his face very ruddy and vivid and his blue eyes shining, dropping his head forwards as he came in, in his usual way, and hesitating in the doorway to watch the inside of the room, keenly and cautiously, before he entered. He was wearing a long-sleeved waistcoat. His face seemed extraordinarily a piece of the out-of-doors come indoors, as holly berries do. In his second of pause in the doorway he took in the two women sitting at table, at opposite ends, saw them sharply. And to his amazement March was dressed in a dress of dull, green silk crêpe. His mouth came open in surprise. If she had suddenly grown a moustache he could not have been more surprised.

"Why," he said, "do you wear a dress, then?"

She looked up, flushing a deep rose colour, and, twisting her mouth with a smile, said:

"Of course I do. What else do you expect me to wear, but a dress?"

"A land girl's uniform, of course," said he.

"Oh," she cried, nonchalant, "that's only for this dirty mucky work about here."

"Isn't it your proper dress, then?" he said.

"No, not indoors, it isn't," she said. But she was blushing all the time as she poured out his tea. He sat down in his chair at table, unable to take his eyes off her. Her dress was a perfectly simple slip of bluey-green crêpe, with a line of gold stitching round the top and round the sleeves, which came to the elbow. It was cut just plain, and round at the top, and showed her white soft throat. Her arms he knew, strong and firm-muscled, for he had often seen her with her sleeves rolled up. But he looked her up and down, up and down.

Banford, at the other end of the table, said not a word, but piggled with the sardine on her plate. He had forgotten her existence. He just simply stared at March, while he ate his bread and margarine in huge mouthfuls, forgetting even his tea.

"Well, I never knew anything make such a difference!" he murmured, across his mouthfuls.

"Oh, goodness!" cried March, blushing still more. "I might be a pink monkey!"

And she rose quickly to her feet and took the teapot to the fire, to the kettle. And as she crouched on the hearth with her green slip about her, the boy stared more wide-eyed than ever. Through the crêpe her woman's form seemed soft and womanly. And when she stood up and walked he saw her legs move soft within her moderately short skirt.

She had on black silk stockings and small patent shoes with little gold buckles.

No, she was another being. She was something quite different. Seeing her always in the hard-cloth breeches, wide on the hips, buttoned on the knee, strong as armour, and in the brown puttees and thick boots, it had never occurred to him that she had a woman's legs and feet. Now it came upon him. She had a woman's soft, skirted legs, and she was accessible. He blushed to the roots of his hair, shoved his nose in his teacup and drank his tea with a little noise that made Banford simply squirm – and strangely, suddenly he felt a man, no longer a youth. He felt a man, with all a man's grave weight of responsibility. A curious quietness and gravity came over his soul. He felt a man, quiet, with a little of the heaviness of male destiny upon him.

She was soft and accessible in her dress. The thought went home in him like an everlasting responsibility.

"Oh for goodness' sake, say something, somebody," cried Banford fretfully. "It might be a funeral." The boy looked at her, and she could not bear his face.

"A funeral!" said March, with a twisted smile. "Why, that breaks my dream."

Suddenly she had thought of Banford in the wood box for a coffin.

"What, have you been dreaming of a wedding?" said Banford sarcastically.

"Must have been," said March.

"Whose wedding?" asked the boy.

"I can't remember," said March.

She was shy and rather awkward that evening, in spite of the fact that, wearing a dress, her bearing was much more subdued than in her uniform. She felt unpeeled and rather exposed. She felt almost improper.

They talked desultorily about Henry's departure next morning, and made the trivial arrangement. But of the matter on their minds, none of them spoke. They were rather quiet and friendly this evening; Banford had practically nothing to say. But inside herself she seemed still, perhaps kindly.

At nine o'clock March brought in the tray with the everlasting tea and a little cold meat which Banford had managed to procure. It was the last supper, so Banford did not want to be disagreeable. She felt a bit sorry for the boy, and felt she must be as nice as she could.

He wanted her to go to bed. She was usually the first. But she sat on in her chair under the lamp, glancing at her book now and then, and staring into the fire. A deep silence had come into the room. It was broken by March asking, in a rather small tone:

"What time is it, Jill?"

"Five past ten," said Banford, looking at her wrist.

And then not a sound. The boy had looked up from the book he was holding between his knees. His rather wide, cat-shaped face had its obstinate look, his eyes were watchful.

"What about bed?" said March at last.

"I'm ready when you are," said Banford.

"Oh, very well," said March. "I'll fill your bottle."

She was as good as her word. When the hot-water bottle was ready, she lit a candle and went upstairs with it. Banford remained in her chair, listening acutely. March came downstairs again.

"There you are then," she said. "Are you going up?"

"Yes, in a minute," said Banford. But the minute passed, and she sat on in her chair under the lamp.

Henry, whose eyes were shining like a cat's as he watched from under his brows, and whose face seemed wider, more chubbed and cat-like with unalterable obstinacy, now rose to his feet to try his throw.

"I think I'll go and look if I can see the she-fox," he said. "She may be creeping round. Won't you come as well for a minute, Nellie, and see if we see anything?"

"Me!" cried March, looking up with her startled, wondering face.

"Yes. Come on," he said. It was wonderful how soft and warm and coaxing his voice could be, how near. The very sound of it made Banford's blood boil. "Come on for a minute," he said, looking down into her uplifted, unsure face.

And she rose to her feet as if drawn up by this young, ruddy face that was looking down on her.

"I should think you're never going out at this time of night, Nellie!" cried Banford.

"Yes, just for a minute," said the boy, looking round on her, and speaking with an odd sharp yelp in his voice.

March looked from one to the other, as if confused, vague. Banford rose to her feet for battle.

"Why, it's ridiculous. It's bitter cold. You'll catch your death in that thin frock. And in those slippers. You're not going to do any such thing."

There was a moment's pause. Banford turtled up like a little fighting cock, facing March and the boy.

"Oh, I don't think you need worry yourself," he replied. "A moment under the stars won't do anybody any damage. I'll get the rug off the sofa in the dining room. You're coming, Nellie."

His voice had so much anger and contempt and fury in it as he spoke to Banford, and so much tenderness and proud authority as he spoke to March, that the latter answered:

"Yes, I'm coming."

And she turned with him to the door.

Banford, standing there in the middle of the room, suddenly burst into a long wail and a spasm of sobs. She covered her face with her poor thin hands, and her thin shoulders shook in an agony of weeping. March looked back from the door.

"Jill!" she cried in a frantic tone, like someone just coming awake. And she seemed to start towards her darling.

But the boy had March's arm in his grip, and she could not move. She did not know why she could not move. It was as in a dream, when the heart strains and the body cannot stir.

"Never mind," said the boy softly. "Let her cry. Let her cry. She will have to cry sooner or later. And the tears will relieve her feelings. They will do her good."

So he drew March slowly through the doorway. But her last look was back to the poor little figure which stood in the middle of the room with covered face and thin shoulders shaken with bitter weeping.

In the dining room he picked up the rug and said:

"Wrap yourself up in this."

She obeyed – and they reached the kitchen door, he holding her soft and firm by the arm, though she did not know it. When she saw the night outside she started back.

"I must go back to Jill," she said. "I *must*! Oh yes, I must."

Her tone sounded final. The boy let go of her and she turned indoors. But he seized her again and arrested her.

"Wait a minute," he said. "Wait a minute. Even if you go you're not going yet."

"Leave go! Leave go!" she cried. "My place is at Jill's side. Poor little thing, she's sobbing her heart out."

"Yes," said the boy bitterly. "And your heart too, and mine as well."

"Your heart?" said March. He still gripped her and detained her.

"Isn't it as good as her heart?" he said. "Or do you think it's not?"

"Your heart?" she said again, incredulous.

"Yes, mine! Mine! Do you think I haven't *got* a heart?" And with his hot grasp he took her hand and pressed it under his left breast. "There's my heart," he said, "if you don't believe in it."

It was wonder which made her attend. And then she felt the deep, heavy, powerful stroke of his heart, terrible, like something from beyond. It was like something from beyond, something awful from outside, signalling to her. And the signal paralysed her. It beat upon her very soul, and made her helpless. She forgot Jill. She could not think of Jill any more. She could not think of her. That terrible signalling from outside!

The boy put his arm round her waist.

"Come with me," he said gently. "Come and let us say what we've got to say."

And he drew her outside, closed the door. And she went with him darkly down the garden path. That he should have a beating heart! And that he should have his arm round her, outside the blanket! She was too confused to think who he was or what he was.

He took her to a dark corner of the shed, where there was a toolbox with a lid, long and low.

"We'll sit here a minute," he said.

And obediently she sat down by his side.

"Give me your hand," he said.

She gave him both her hands, and he held them between his own. He was young, and it made him tremble.

"You'll marry me. You'll marry me before I go back, won't you?" he pleaded.

"Why, aren't we both a pair of fools?" she said.

He had put her in the corner, so that she should not look out and see the lit window of the house, across the dark garden. He tried to keep her all there inside the shed with him.

"In what way a pair of fools?" he said. "If you go back to Canada with me, I've got a job and a good wage waiting for me, and it's a nice place, near the mountains. Why shouldn't you marry me? Why shouldn't we marry? I should like to have you there with me. I should like to feel I'd got somebody there, at the back of me, all my life."

"You'd easily find somebody else who'd suit you better," she said.

"Yes, I might easily find another girl. I know I could. But not one I really wanted. I've never met one I really wanted for good. You see, I'm thinking of all my life. If I marry, I want to feel it's for all my life. Other girls: well, they're just girls, nice enough to go a walk with now and then. Nice enough for a bit of play. But when I think of my life, then I should be very sorry to have to marry one of them, I should indeed."

"You mean they wouldn't make you a good wife."

"Yes, I mean that. But I don't mean they wouldn't do their duty by me. I mean – I don't know what I mean. Only when I think of my life, and of you, then the two things go together."

"And what if they didn't?" she said, with her odd sardonic touch.

"Well, I think they would."

They sat for some time silent. He held her hands in his, but he did not make love to her. Since he had realized that she was a woman, and vulnerable, accessible, a certain heaviness had possessed his soul. He did not want to make love to her. He shrank from any such performance, almost with fear. She was a woman, and vulnerable, accessible to him finally, and he held back from that which was ahead, almost with dread. It was a kind of darkness he knew he would enter finally, but of which he did not want as yet even to think. She was the woman, and he was responsible for the strange vulnerability he had suddenly realized in her.

"No," she said at last, "I'm a fool. I know I'm a fool."

"What for?" he asked.

"To go on with this business."

"Do you mean me?" he asked.

"No, I mean myself, I'm making a fool of myself, and a big one."

"Why, because you don't want to marry me, really?"

"Oh, I don't know whether I'm against it, as a matter of fact. That's just it. I don't know."

He looked at her in the darkness, puzzled. He did not in the least know what she meant.

"And don't you know whether you like to sit here with me this minute, or not?" he asked.

"No, I don't really. I don't know whether I wish I was somewhere else, or whether I like being here. I don't know, really."

"Do you wish you were with Miss Banford? Do you wish you'd gone to bed with her?" he asked, as a challenge.

She waited a long time before she answered.

"No," she said at last. "I don't wish that."

"And do you think you would spend all your life with her – when your hair goes white and you are old?" he said.

"No," she said, without much hesitation. "I don't see Jill and me two old women together."

"And don't you think, when I'm an old man, and you're an old woman, we might be together still, as we are now?" he said.

"Well, not as we are now," she replied. "But I could imagine – no, I can't. I can't imagine you an old man. Besides, it's dreadful!"

"What, to be an old man?"

"Yes, of course."

"Not when the time comes," he said. "But it hasn't come. Only it will. And when it does, I should like to think you'd be there as well."

"Sort of old-age pensions," she said drily.

Her kind of witless humour always startled him. He never knew what she meant. Probably she didn't quite know herself.

"No," he said, hurt.

"I don't know why you harp on old age," she said. "I'm not ninety."

"Did anybody ever say you were?" he asked, offended.

They were silent for some time, pulling different ways in the silence.

"I don't want you to make fun of me," he said.

"Don't you?" she replied, enigmatic.

"No, because just this minute I'm serious. And when I'm serious, I believe in not making fun of it."

"You mean nobody else can make fun of you," she replied.

"Yes, I mean that. And I mean I don't believe in making fun of it myself. When it comes over me so that I'm serious, then – there it is, I don't want it to be laughed at."

She was silent for some time. Then she said, in a vague, almost pained voice:

"No, I'm not laughing at you."

A hot wave rose in his heart.

"You believe me, don't you?" he asked.

"Yes, I believe you," she replied, with a twang of her old tired nonchalance, as if she gave in because she was tired. But he didn't care. His heart was hot and clamorous.

"So you agree to marry me before I go? Perhaps at Christmas?"

"Yes, I agree."

"There!" he exclaimed. "That's settled it."

And he sat silent, unconscious, with all the blood burning in all his veins, like fire in all the branches and twigs of him. He only pressed her two hands to his chest, without knowing. When the curious passion began to die down, he seemed to come awake to the world.

"We'll go in, shall we?" he said, as if he realized it was cold.

She rose without answering.

"Kiss me before we go, now you've said it," he said.

And he kissed her gently on the mouth, with a young frightened kiss. It made her feel so young, too, and frightened, and wondering, and tired, tired, as if she were going to sleep.

They went indoors. And in the sitting room, there, crouched by the fire like a queer little witch, was Banford. She looked round with reddened eyes as they entered, but did not rise. He thought she looked frightening, unnatural, crouching there and looking round at them. Evil he thought her look was, and he crossed his fingers.

Banford saw the ruddy, elate face of the youth: he seemed strangely tall and bright and looming. And March had a delicate look on her face – she wanted to hide her face, to screen it, to let it not be seen.

"You've come at last," said Banford uglily.

"Yes, we've come," said he.

"You've been long enough for anything," she said.

"Yes, we have. We've settled it. We shall marry as soon as possible," he replied.

"Oh, you've settled it, have you! Well, I hope you won't live to repent it," said Banford.

"I hope so too," he replied.

"Are you going to bed *now*, Nellie?" said Banford.

"Yes, I'm going now."

"Then for goodness' sake come along."

March looked at the boy. He was glancing with his very bright eyes at her and at Banford. March looked at him wistfully. She wished she could stay with him. She wished she had married him already and it was all over. For oh, she felt suddenly so safe with him. She felt so strangely safe and peaceful in his presence. If only she could sleep in his shelter, and not with Jill. She felt afraid of Jill. In her dim, tender state, it was agony to have to go with Jill and sleep with her. She wanted the boy to save her. She looked again at him.

And he, watching with bright eyes, divined something of what she felt. It puzzled and distressed him that she must go with Jill.

"I shan't forget what you've promised," he said, looking clear into her eyes, right into her eyes, so that he seemed to occupy all herself with his queer, bright look.

She smiled to him faintly, gently. She felt safe again – safe with him.

But in spite of all the boy's precautions, he had a setback. The morning he was leaving the farm, he got March to accompany him to the market town, about six miles away, where they went to the registrar and had their names stuck up as two people who were going to marry. He was to come at Christmas, and the wedding was to take place then. He hoped in the spring to be able to take March back to Canada with him, now the War was really over. Though he was so young, he had saved some money.

"You never have to be without *some* money at the back of you, if you can help it," he said.

So she saw him off in the train that was going west – his camp was on Salisbury Plain. And with big dark eyes she watched him go, and it seemed as if everything real in life was retreating as the train retreated with his queer, chubby, ruddy face, that seemed so broad across the cheeks, and which never seemed to change its expression, save when a cloud of sulky anger hung on the brow, or the bright eyes fixed themselves in their stare. This was what happened now. He leant there out of the carriage window as the train drew off, saying goodbye and staring back at her, but his face quite unchanged. There was no emotion on his face. Only his eyes tightened and became fixed and intent in their watching, as a cat when suddenly she sees something and stares. So the boy's eyes stared fixedly as the train drew away, and she was left feeling intensely forlorn. Failing his physical presence, she seemed to have nothing of him. And she had nothing of anything. Only his face was fixed in her mind: the full, ruddy, unchanging cheeks, and the straight snout of a nose, and the two eyes staring above. All she could remember was how he suddenly wrinkled his nose when he laughed, as a puppy does when he is playfully growling. But him, himself, and what he was – she knew nothing, she had nothing of him when he left her.

On the ninth day after he had left her, he received this letter.

Dear Henry,

I have been over it all again in my mind, this business of me and you, and it seems to me impossible. When you aren't there I see what a fool I am. When you are there you seem to blind me to things as they actually are. You make me see things all unreal and I don't know what. Then when I am alone again with Jill I seem to come to my own senses and realize what a fool I am making of myself and how I am treating you unfairly. Because it must be unfair to you for me to go on with this affair when I can't feel in my heart that I really love you. I know people talk a lot of stuff and nonsense about love, and I don't want to do that. I want to keep to plain facts and act in a sensible way. And that seems to me what I'm not doing. I don't see on what grounds I am going to marry you. I know I am not head over heels in love with you, as I have fancied myself to be with fellows when I was a young fool of a girl. You are an absolute stranger to me, and it seems to me you will always be one. So on what grounds am I going to marry you? When I think of Jill she is ten times more real to me. I know her and I'm awfully fond of her, and I hate myself for a beast if I ever hurt her little finger. We have a life together. And even if it can't last for ever, it is a life while it does last. And it might last as long as either of us lives. Who knows how long we've got to live? She is a delicate little thing, perhaps nobody but me knows how delicate. And as for me, I feel I might fall down the well any day. What I don't seem to see at all is you. When I think of what I've been and what I've done with you I'm afraid I am a few screws loose. I should be sorry to think that softening of the brain is setting in so soon, but that is what it seems like. You are such an absolute stranger and so different from what I'm used to and we don't seem to have a thing in common. As for love, the word seems impossible. I know what love means even in Jill's case, and I know that in this affair with you it's an absolute impossibility. And then going to Canada. I'm sure I must have been clean off my chump when I promised such a thing. It makes me feel fairly frightened of myself. I feel I might do something really silly that I wasn't responsible for – and end my days in a lunatic asylum. You may think that's all

I'm fit for after the way I've gone on, but it isn't a very nice thought for me. Thank goodness Jill is here and her being here makes me feel sane again, else I don't know what I might do, I might have an accident with the gun one evening. I love Jill and she makes me feel safe and sane, with her loving anger against me for being such a fool. Well, what I want to say is won't you let us cry the whole thing off? I can't marry you, and really, I won't do such a thing if it seems to me wrong. It is all a great mistake. I've made a complete fool of myself, and all I can do is to apologize to you and ask you please to forget it and please to take no further notice of me. Your fox skin is nearly ready and seems all right. I will post it to you if you will let me know if this address is still right, and if you will accept my apology for the awful and lunatic way I have behaved with you, and then let the matter rest.

Jill sends her kindest regards. Her mother and father are staying with us over Christmas.

Yours very sincerely,
Ellen March

The boy read this letter in camp as he was cleaning his kit. He set his teeth and for a moment went almost pale, yellow round the eyes with fury. He said nothing and saw nothing and felt nothing but a livid rage that was quite unreasoning. Balked! Balked again! Balked! He wanted the woman, he had fixed like doom upon having her. He felt that was his doom, his destiny and his reward, to have this woman. She was his heaven and hell on earth, and he would have none elsewhere. Sightless with rage and thwarted madness he got through the morning. Save that in his mind he was lurking and scheming towards an issue, he would have committed some insane act. Deep in himself he felt like roaring and howling and gnashing his teeth and breaking things. But he was too intelligent. He knew society was on top of him, and he must scheme. So with his teeth bitten together and his nose curiously slightly lifted, like some creature that is vicious, and his eyes fixed and staring, he went through the morning's affairs drunk with anger and suppression. In his mind was one thing – Banford. He took no heed of all March's outpouring – none. One thorn rankled, stuck in his mind. Banford. In his mind, in his soul, in his whole being, one thorn rankling to insanity. And he would have to get it out. He would have to get it out. He would have to get the thorn of Banford out of his life if he died for it.

With this one fixed idea in his mind, he went to ask for twenty-four hours' leave of absence. He knew it was not due to him. His consciousness was supernaturally keen. He knew where he must go – he must go to the Captain. But how could he get at the Captain? In that great camp of wooden huts and tents he had no idea where his Captain was.

But he went to the officers' canteen. There was his captain standing talking with three other officers. Henry stood in the doorway at attention.

"May I speak to Captain Berryman?" The Captain was Cornish like himself.

"What do you want?" called the Captain.

"May I speak to you, Captain?"

"What do you want?" replied the Captain, not stirring from among his group of fellow officers.

Henry watched his superior for a minute without speaking.

"You won't refuse me, sir, will you?" he asked gravely.

"It depends what it is."

"Can I have twenty-four hours' leave?"

"No, you've no business to ask."

"I know I haven't. But I must ask you."

"You've had your answer."

"Don't send me away, Captain."

There was something strange about the boy as he stood there so everlasting in the doorway. The Cornish captain felt the strangeness at once, and eyed him shrewdly.

"Why? What's afoot?" he said, curious.

"I'm in trouble about something. I must go to Blewbury," said the boy.

"Blewbury, eh? After the girls?"

"Yes, it is a woman, Captain." And the boy, as he stood there with his head reaching forwards a little, went suddenly terribly pale, or yellow, and his lips seemed to give off pain. The Captain saw and paled a little also. He turned aside.

"Go on then," he said. "But for God's sake don't cause any trouble of any sort."

"I won't, Captain, thank you."

He was gone. The Captain, upset, took a gin-and-bitters. Henry managed to hire a bicycle. It was twelve o'clock when he left the camp.

He had sixty miles of wet and muddy crossroads to ride. But he was in the saddle and down the road without a thought of food.

At the farm, March was busy with a work she had had some time in hand. A bunch of Scotch fir trees stood at the end of the open shed, on a little bank where ran the fences between two of the gorse-shaggy meadows. The furthest of these trees was dead – it had died in the summer and stood with all its needles brown and sere in the air. It was not a very big tree. And it was absolutely dead. So March determined to have it, although they were not allowed to cut any of the timber. But it would make such splendid firing in these days of scarce fuel.

She had been giving a few stealthy chops at the trunk for a week or more, every now and then hacking away for five minutes, low down, near the ground, so no one should notice. She had not tried the saw, it was such hard work alone. Now the tree stood with a great yawning gap in his base, perched as it were on one sinew, and ready to fall. But he did not fall.

It was late in the damp December afternoon, with cold mists creeping out of the woods and up the hollows, and darkness waiting to sink in from above. There was a bit of yellowness where the sun was fading away beyond the low woods of the distance. March took her axe and went to the tree. The small thud-thud of her blows resounded rather ineffectual about the wintry homestead. Banford came out wearing her thick coat, but with no hat on her head, so that her thin, bobbed hair blew on the uneasy wind that sounded in the pines and in the wood.

"What I'm afraid of," said Banford, "is that it will fall on the shed and we s'll have another job repairing that."

"Oh, I don't think so," said March, straightening herself, and wiping her arm over her hot brow. She was flushed red, her eyes were very wide – open and queer, her upper lip lifted away from her two white front teeth with a curious, almost rabbit-look.

A little stout man in a black overcoat and a bowler hat came pottering across the yard. He had a pink face and a white beard and smallish, pale-blue eyes. He was not very old, but nervy, and he walked with little short steps.

"What do you think, Father?" said Banford. "Don't you think it might hit the shed in falling?"

"Shed, no!" said the man. "Can't hit the shed. Might as well say the fence."

"The fence doesn't matter," said March, in her high voice.

"Wrong as usual, am I!" said Banford, wiping her straying hair from her eyes.

The tree stood as it were on one spelch of itself, leaning, and creaking in the wind. It grew on the bank of a little dry ditch between the two meadows. On the top of the bank straggled one fence, running to the bushes uphill. Several trees clustered there in the corner of the field near the shed and near the gate which led into the yard. Towards this gate, horizontal across the weary meadows, came the grassy, rutted approach from the high road. There trailed another rickety fence, long split poles joining the short, thick, wide-apart uprights.

The three people stood at the back of the gate, in the corner of the shed meadow, just above the yard gate. The house with its two gables and its porch stood tidy in a little grassed garden across the yard. A little stout rosy-faced woman in a little red woollen shoulder shawl had come and taken her stand in the porch.

"Isn't it down yet?" she cried, in a high little voice.

"Just thinking about it," called her husband. His tone towards the two girls was always rather mocking and satirical. March did not want to go on with her hitting while he was there. As for him, he wouldn't lift a stick from the ground if he could help it, complaining, like his daughter, of rheumatics in his shoulder. So the three stood there a moment silent in the cold afternoon, in the bottom corner near the yard.

They heard the far-off taps of a gate, and craned to look. Away across, on the green horizontal approach, a figure was just swinging onto a bicycle again, and lurching up and down over the grass, approaching.

"Why it's one of our boys – it's Jack," said the old man.

"Can't be," said Banford.

March craned her head to look. She alone recognized the khaki figure. She flushed, but said nothing.

"No, it isn't Jack, I don't think," said the old man, staring with little round blue eyes under his white lashes.

In another moment the bicycle lurched into sight, and the rider dropped off at the gate. It was Henry, his face wet and red and spotted with mud. He was altogether a muddy sight.

"Oh!" cried Banford, as if afraid. "Why, it's Henry!"

"What!" muttered the old man. He had a thick, rapid, muttering way of speaking, and was slightly deaf. "What? What? Who is it? Who is it do you say? That young fellow? That young fellow of Nellie's? Oh! Oh!" And the satiric smile came on his pink face and white eyelashes.

Henry, pushing the wet hair off his steaming brow, had caught sight of them and heard what the old man said. His hot young face seemed to flame in the cold light.

"Oh, are you all there!" he said, giving his sudden, puppy's little laugh. He was so hot and dazed with cycling he hardly knew where he was. He leant the bicycle against the fence and climbed over into the corner onto the bank, without going into the yard.

"Well, I must say, we weren't expecting *you*," said Banford laconically.

"No, I suppose not," said he, looking at March.

She stood aside, slack, with one knee drooped and the axe resting its head loosely on the ground. Her eyes were wide and vacant, and her upper lip lifted from her teeth in that helpless, fascinated rabbit-look. The moment she saw his glowing red face it was all over with her. She was as helpless as if she had been bound. The moment she saw the way his head seemed to reach forwards.

"Well, who is it? Who is it, anyway?" asked the smiling, satiric old man in his muttering voice.

"Why, Mr Grenfel, whom you've heard us tell about, Father," said Banford coldly.

"Heard you tell about, I should think so. Heard of nothing else, practically," muttered the elderly man, with his queer little jeering smile on his face. "How do you do," he added, suddenly reaching out his hand to Henry.

The boy shook hands, just as startled. Then the two men fell apart.

"Cycled over from Salisbury Plain have you?" asked the old man.

"Yes."

"Hm! Longish ride. How long d'it take you, eh? Some time, eh? Several hours, I suppose."

"About four."

"Eh! Four! Yes, I should have thought so. When are you going back then?"

"I've got till tomorrow evening."

"Till tomorrow evening, eh? Yes. Hm. Girls weren't expecting you, were they?"

And the old man turned his pale-blue, round little eyes under their white lashes mockingly towards the girls. Henry also looked round. He had become a little awkward. He looked at March, who was still staring away into the distance, as if to see where the cattle were. Her hand was on the pommel of the axe, whose head rested loosely on the ground.

"What were you doing there?" he asked in his soft, courteous voice. "Cutting a tree down?"

March seemed not to hear, as if in a trance.

"Yes," said Banford. "We've been at it for over a week."

"Oh! And have you done it all by yourselves then?"

"Nellie's done it all, I've done nothing," said Banford.

"Really! You must have worked quite hard," he said, addressing himself in a curious gentle tone direct to March. She did not answer, but remained half averted, staring away towards the woods above as if in a trance.

"*Nellie!*" cried Banford sharply. "Can't you answer?"

"What – me?" cried March, starting round, and looking from one to the other. "Did anyone speak to me?"

"Dreaming!" muttered the old man, turning aside to smile. "Must be in love, eh, dreaming in the daytime!"

"Did you say anything to me?" said March, looking at the boy as from a strange distance, her eyes wide and doubtful, her face delicately flushed.

"I said you must have worked hard at the tree," he replied courteously.

"Oh, that! Bit by bit. I thought it would have come down by now."

"I'm thankful it hasn't come down in the night, to frighten us to death," said Banford.

"Let me just finish it for you, shall I?" said the boy.

March slanted the axe shaft in his direction.

"Would you like to?" she said.

"Yes, if you wish it," he said.

"Oh, I'm thankful when the thing's down, that's all," she replied, nonchalant.

"Which way is it going to fall?" said Banford. "Will it hit the shed?"

"No, it won't hit the shed," he said. "I should think it will fall there – quite clear. Though it might give a twist and catch the fence."

"Catch the fence!" cried the old man. "What, catch the fence! When it's leaning at that angle? Why it's further off than the shed. It won't catch the fence."

"No," said Henry, "I don't suppose it will. It has plenty of room to fall quite clear, and I suppose it will fall clear."

"Won't tumble backwards on top of *us*, will it?" asked the old man, sarcastic.

"No, it won't do that," said Henry, taking off his short overcoat and his tunic. "Ducks! Ducks! Go back!"

A line of four brown-specked ducks led by a brown-and-green drake were stemming away downhill from the upper meadow, coming like boats running on a ruffled sea, cackling their way top speed downwards towards the fence and towards the little group of people, and cackling as excitedly as if they brought the news of the Spanish Armada.

"Silly things! Silly things!" cried Banford, going forwards to turn them off. But they came eagerly towards her, opening their yellow-green beaks and quacking as if they were so excited to say something.

"There's no food. There's nothing here. You must wait a bit," said Banford to them. "Go away. Go away. Go round to the yard."

They didn't go, so she climbed the fence to swerve them round under the gate and into the yard. So off they waggled in an excited string once more, wagging their rumps like the stems of little gondolas, ducking under the bar of the gate. Banford stood on the top of the bank, just over the fence, looking down on the other three.

Henry looked up at her, and met her queer, round-pupilled, weak eyes staring behind her spectacles. He was perfectly still. He looked away, up at the weak, leaning tree. And as he looked into the sky, like a huntsman who is watching a flying bird, he thought to himself, "If the tree falls in just such a way, and spins just so much as it falls, then the branch there will strike her exactly as she stands on top of that bank."

He looked at her again. She was wiping the hair from her brow again, with that perpetual gesture. In his heart he had decided her death. A terrible force still seemed in him, and a power that was just his. If he turned even a hair's breadth in the wrong direction, he would lose the power.

"Mind yourself, Miss Banford," he said. And his heart held perfectly still, in the terrible pure will that she should not move.

"Who, me, mind myself?" she cried, her father's jeering tone in her voice. "Why, do you think you might hit me with the axe?"

"No, it's just possible the tree might, though," he answered soberly. But the tone of his voice seemed to her to imply that he was only being falsely solicitous and trying to make her move because it was his will to move her.

"Absolutely impossible," she said.

He heard her. But he held himself icy still, lest he should lose his power.

"No, it's just possible. You'd better come down this way."

"Oh, all right. Let us see some crack Canadian tree-felling," she retorted.

"Ready then," he said, taking the axe, looking round to see he was clear.

There was a moment of pure, motionless suspense, when the world seemed to stand still. Then suddenly his form seemed to flash up enormously tall and fearful, he gave two swift, flashing blows in immediate succession, the tree was severed, turning slowly, spinning strangely in the air, and coming down like a sudden darkness on the earth. No one saw what was happening except himself. No one heard the strange little cry which Banford gave as the dark end of the bough swooped down, down on her. No one saw her crouch a little and receive the blow on the back of the neck. No one saw her flung outwards and laid, a little twitching heap, at the foot of the fence. No one except the boy. And he watched with intense bright eyes, as he would watch a wild goose he had shot. Was it winged or dead? Dead!

Immediately he gave a loud cry. Immediately March gave a wild shriek that went far, far down the afternoon. And the father started a strange bellowing sound.

The boy leapt the fence and ran to the figure. The back of the neck and head was a mass of blood, of horror. He turned it over. The body was quivering with little convulsions. But she was dead really. He knew it, that it was so. He knew it in his soul and his blood. The inner necessity of his life was fulfilling itself, it was he who was to live. The thorn was drawn out of his bowels. So he put her down gently; she was dead.

He stood up. March was standing there, petrified and absolutely motionless. Her face was dead white, her eyes big black pools. The old man was scrambling horribly over the fence.

"I'm afraid it's killed her," said the boy.

The old man was making curious, blubbering noises as he huddled over the fence.

"What!" cried March, starting electric.

"Yes, I'm afraid," repeated the boy.

March was coming forwards. The boy was over the fence before she reached it.

"What do you say, killed her?" she asked in a sharp voice.

"I'm afraid so," he answered softly.

She went still whiter, fearful. The two stood facing one another. Her black eyes gazed on him with the last look of resistance. And then in a last agonized failure she began to grizzle, to cry in a shivery little fashion of a child that doesn't want to cry, but which is beaten from within, and gives that little first shudder of sobbing which is not yet weeping, dry and fearful.

He had won. She stood there absolutely helpless, shuddering her dry sobs and her mouth trembling rapidly. And then, as in a child, with a little crash came the tears and the blind agony of sightless weeping. She sank down on the grass and sat there with her hands on her breast, and her face lifted in sightless, convulsed weeping. He stood above her, looking down on her, mute, pale and everlasting seeming. He never moved, but looked down on her. And among all the torture of the scene, the torture of his own heart and bowels, he was glad; he had won.

After a long time he stooped to her and took her hands.

"Don't cry," he said softly. "Don't cry."

She looked up at him with tears running from her eyes, a senseless look of helplessness and submission. So she gazed on him as if sightless, yet looking up to him. She would never leave him again. He had won her. And he knew it and was glad, because he wanted her for his life. His life must have her. And now he had won her. It was what his life must have.

But if he had won her, he had not yet got her. They were married at Christmas as he had planned, and he got again ten days' leave. They went to Cornwall, to his own village, on the sea. He realized that it was awful for her to be at the farm any more.

But though she belonged to him, though she lived in his shadow, as if she could not be away from him, she was not happy. She did not want to leave him, and yet she did not feel free with him. Everything round her seemed to watch her, seemed to press on her. He had won her, he had her with him, she was his wife. And she – she belonged to him, she knew it. But she was not glad. And he was still foiled. He realized that though he was married to her and possessed her in every possible way, apparently, and though she *wanted* him to possess her, she wanted it, she wanted nothing else now, still he did not quite succeed.

Something was missing. Instead of her soul swaying with new life, it seemed to droop, to bleed, as if it were wounded. She would sit for a long time with her hand in his, looking away at the sea. And in her dark, vacant eyes was a sort of wound, and her face looked a little peaked. If he spoke to her, she would turn to him with a faint new smile, the strange, quivering little smile of a woman who has died in the old way of love, and can't quite rise to the new way. She still felt she ought to *do* something, to strain herself in some direction. And there was nothing to do, and no direction in which to strain herself. And she could not quite accept the submergence which his new love put upon her. If she was in love, she ought to *exert* herself, in some way, loving. She felt the weary need of our day to *exert* herself in love. But she knew that in fact she must no more exert herself in love. He would not have the love which exerted itself towards him. It made his brow go black. No, he wouldn't let her exert her love towards him. No, she had to be passive, to acquiesce and to be submerged under the surface of love. She had to be like the seaweeds she saw as she peered down from the boat, swaying forever delicately underwater, with all their delicate fibrils put tenderly out upon the flood, sensitive, utterly sensitive and receptive within the shadowy sea, and never, never rising and looking forth above water while they lived. Never. Never looking forth from the water until they died, only then washing, corpses, upon the surface. But while they lived, always submerged, always beneath the wave. Beneath the wave they might have powerful roots, stronger than iron, they might be tenacious and dangerous in their soft waving within the flood. Beneath the water they might be stronger, more indestructible than resistant oak trees are on land. But it was always underwater, always underwater. And she, being a woman, must be like that.

And she had been so used to the very opposite. She had had to take all the thought for love and for life, and all the responsibility. Day after day she had been responsible for the coming day, for the coming year, for her dear Jill's health and happiness and well-being. Verily, in her own small way, she had felt herself responsible for the well-being of the world. And this had been her great stimulant, this grand feeling that, in her own small sphere, she was responsible for the well-being of the world.

And she had failed. She knew that, even in her small way, she had failed. She had failed to satisfy her own feeling of responsibility. It was so difficult. It seemed so grand and easy at first. And the more you tried, the more difficult it became. It had seemed so easy to make one beloved creature happy. And the more you tried, the worse the failure. It was terrible. She had been all her life reaching, reaching, and what she reached for seemed so near, until she had stretched to her utmost limit. And then it was always beyond her.

Always beyond her, vaguely, unrealizably beyond her, and she was left with nothingness at last. The life she reached for, the happiness she reached for, the well-being she reached for all slipped back, became unreal, the further she stretched her hand. She wanted some goal, some finality – and there was none. Always this ghastly reaching, reaching, striving for something that might be just beyond. Even to make Jill happy. She was glad Jill was dead. For she had realized that she could never make her happy. Jill would always be fretting herself thinner and thinner, weaker and weaker. Her pains grew worse instead of less. It would be so for ever. She was glad she was dead.

And if she had married a man it would have been just the same. The woman striving, striving to make the man happy, striving within her own limits for the well-being of her world. And always achieving failure. Little, foolish successes in money or in ambition. But at the very point where she most wanted success in the anguished effort to make some one beloved human being happy and perfect, there the failure was almost catastrophic. You wanted to make your beloved happy, and his happiness seemed always achievable. If only you did just this, that and the other. And you did this, that and the other, in all good faith, and every time the failure became a little more ghastly. You could love yourself to ribbons, and strive and strain yourself to the bone, and things would go from bad to worse, bad to worse, as far as happiness went. The awful mistake of happiness.

Poor March, in her goodwill and her responsibility, she had strained herself till it seemed to her that the whole of her life and everything was only a horrible abyss of nothingness. The more you reached after the fatal flower of happiness which trembles so blue and lovely in a crevice just beyond your grasp, the more fearfully you became aware of the ghastly and awful gulf of the precipice below you, into which you will inevitably plunge, as into the bottomless pit, if you reach any further. You pluck flower after flower – it is never *the* flower. The flower itself – its calyx is a horrible gulf, it is the bottomless pit.

That is the whole history of the search for happiness, whether it be your own or somebody else's that you want to win. It ends, and it always ends, in the ghastly sense of the bottomless nothingness into which you will inevitably fall if you strain any further.

And women? What goal can any woman achieve, except happiness? Just happiness, for herself and the whole world. That, and nothing else. And so, she assumes the responsibility and sets off towards her goal. She can see it there, at the foot of the rainbow. Or she can see it a little way beyond, in the blue distance. Not far, not far.

But the end of the rainbow is a bottomless gulf down which you can fall for ever without arriving, and the blue distance is a void pit which can swallow you and all your efforts into its emptiness, and still be no emptier. You and all your efforts. So, the illusion of attainable happiness!

Poor March, she had set off so wonderfully towards the blue goal. And the further and further she had gone, the more fearful had become the realization of emptiness. An agony, an insanity at last.

She was glad it was over. She was glad to sit on the shore and look westwards over the sea, and know the great strain had ended. She would never strain for love and happiness any more. And Jill was safely dead. Poor Jill, poor Jill. It must be sweet to be dead.

For her own part, death was not her destiny. She would have to leave her destiny to the boy. But then, the boy. He wanted more than that. He wanted her to give herself without defences, to sink and become submerged in him. And she – she wanted to sit still, like a woman on the last milestone, and watch. She wanted to see, to know, to understand. She wanted to be alone, with him at her side.

And he! He did not want her to watch any more, to see any more, to understand any more. He wanted to veil her woman's spirit, as Orientals veil the woman's face. He wanted her to commit herself to him, and to put her independent spirit to sleep. He wanted to take away from her all her effort, all that seemed her very *raison d'être*. He wanted to make her submit, yield, blindly pass away out of all her strenuous consciousness. He wanted to take away her consciousness, and make her just his woman. Just his woman.

And she was so tired, so tired, like a child that wants to go to sleep, but which fights against sleep as if sleep were death. She seemed to stretch her eyes wider in the obstinate effort and tension of keeping awake. She *would* keep awake. She *would* know. She *would* consider and judge and decide. She *would* have the reins of her own life between her own hands. She *would* be an independent woman to the last. But she was so tired, so tired of everything. And sleep seemed near. And there was such rest in the boy.

Yet there, sitting in a niche of the high west cliffs of West Cornwall, looking over the westward sea, she stretched her eyes wider and wider. Away to the west, Canada, America. She *would* know and she *would* see what was ahead. And the boy, sitting beside her, staring down at the gulls, had a cloud between his brows and the strain of discontent in his eyes. He wanted her asleep, at peace in him. He wanted her at peace, asleep in him. And *there* she was, dying with the strain of her own wakefulness. Yet she would not sleep: no, never. Sometimes he thought bitterly that he ought to have left her. He ought never to have killed Banford. He should have left Banford and March to kill one another.

But that was only impatience, and he knew it. He was waiting, waiting to go west. He was aching almost in torment to leave England, to go west, to take March away. To leave this shore! He believed that as they crossed the seas, as they left this England which he so hated, because in some way it seemed to have stung him with poison, she would go to sleep. She would close her eyes at last, and give in to him.

And then he would have her, and he would have his own life at last. He chafed, feeling he hadn't got his own life. He would never have it till she yielded and slept in him. Then he would have all his own life as a young man and a male, and she would have all her own life as a woman and a female. There would be no more of this awful straining. She would not be a man any more, an independent woman with a man's responsibility. Nay, even the responsibility for her own soul she would have to commit to him. He knew it was so, and obstinately held out against her, waiting for the surrender.

"You'll feel better when once we get over the seas, to Canada, over there," he said to her, as they sat among the rocks on the cliff. She looked away to the sea's horizon, as if it were not real. Then she looked round at him, with the strained, strange look of a child that is struggling against sleep.

"Shall I?" she said.

"Yes," he answered quietly.

And her eyelids dropped with the slow motion, sleep weighing them unconscious. But she pulled them open again to say:

"Yes, I may. I can't tell. I can't tell what it will be like over there."

"If only we could go soon!" he said, with pain in his voice.

Note on the Text

The text in the present edition is based on the first edition published in 1923, edited by Dieter Mehl. The spelling and punctuation have been standardized, modernized and made consistent throughout.

Extra Material

on

D.H. Lawrence's

The Fox

D.H. Lawrence's Life

David Herbert Lawrence was born on 11th September 1885 *Birth and Early Life* in Eastwood, a small colliery town just outside Nottingham. He was the fourth of five children – three brothers and two sisters. His father and most of his other relatives were involved in some capacity with work at one of the collieries, including labour at the coal-face.

His mother Lydia had once had ambitions to be a teacher, but the poverty of her parents had thwarted these early aspirations. However, she still took an interest in reading and intellectual matters. She tried to contribute to the Lawrence family income by running a small clothes shop from the ground floor of the family house – a financial venture which was never very successful. Lydia tried to encourage all of her children to save money and study, but Arthur, her husband, would go out drinking most evenings, leading to arguments and tension.

The boys in the local school were almost all destined to finish up down the mine, while the girls would work in the colliery canteens and laundries. However, from an early age the Lawrence children seemed to aim for higher things, and took their school studies extremely seriously. Furthermore, they regularly attended the local Nonconformist Christian chapel, and all took the pledge early in their lives not to touch alcohol.

A major dramatic occurrence in D.H. Lawrence's early life *Bereavement and Illness* was the death in 1901 of his elder brother Ernest from erysipelas. After this traumatic experience, Lawrence developed severe pneumonia and nearly died. This may have been a contributing factor to the tuberculosis and general ill health which dogged his later years, and finally caused his death.

Teaching Career Lawrence was at the time reading omnivorously in the local municipal library and at school. In 1902 he became a pupil teacher at a senior school in Eastwood – a common arrangement at the time. Some of the more promising older pupils were given lessons by the headmaster early in the mornings, and then they proceeded to teach the other pupils, usually for nothing or a nominal sum, since the personal tuition they received was meant to constitute their reward. Lawrence's token recompense was £12 per year. He took the opportunity of spending some time each week at what would now be called "teachers' centres" in Nottingham and at Ilkeston in Derbyshire, which ran training courses for other people in his situation living in the area; this led to a huge expansion of his social and intellectual horizons.

After two years as a pupil teacher, Lawrence successfully sat the King's Scholarship Examination in 1904, which gave him entry to a teacher-training college, or even, if he so wished, the opportunity to study for a degree at a university – almost unheard of at the time for anybody from a lower-class background. Interviews with this "working-class boy made good" were subsequently published in the local press and in the national teachers' magazines *The Schoolmaster* and *The Teacher*.

Although success in the examination conferred access to higher education, it gave little financial assistance, and so Lawrence and his family now had to decide whether he should do the degree full-time, supported by his family, or part-time, working to finance himself, as there were no student grants at the time.

It was finally decided he should spend a further year as a pupil teacher at a salary of £50 per year before going to university to do his teacher training. He entered the teacher-training department of Nottingham University in September 1906, but between the scholarship examination and entry to higher education he had started to write. He experimented with poetry, and in 1906 began writing *Laetitia*, the earliest version of his first published novel, *The White Peacock*.

Jessie Chambers Lawrence was by now spending a considerable amount of time in the company of a young woman he had met some five years earlier, Jessie Chambers. They read together and discussed literature, philosophy and other intellectual subjects. His sisters and mother were worried that this blossoming relationship would be a distraction to "Bert"; they wanted him and Jessie either to get engaged, or meet less frequently. Lawrence took all this to heart, and told Jessie they must cut down the number of their meetings drastically for the time being. She was deeply hurt, and this was the first of numerous occasions on which he treated Jessie, and other women, with seeming insensitivity and selfishness.

At teacher-training college, Lawrence met socialists and *Early Writing* freethinkers, and his whole universe expanded. He spent a great deal of time writing and revising his novel. He found the course boring, but ploughed ahead with it and finally gained his teaching certificate in 1908. He also wrote more poetry and experimented with short-story-writing. He submitted three stories to a competition in the biggest Nottingham newspaper, and one of these – 'The Prelude' – submitted for him by Jessie Chambers under her own name – won the prize for best story in its category and was printed in the paper. Lawrence also apparently sent some work – possibly one or more essays or sketches – to G.K. Chesterton, then literary editor at the *Daily News* in London, but these were returned with such negative comments that he nearly decided to give up writing altogether.

Lawrence was still living at home but, under the influence of the new ideas he was encountering at college, he began to react against his narrow upbringing, particularly the world of the Nonconformist chapel his parents attended, and religion in general. Unlike his fellow graduates, Lawrence was prepared to bide his time waiting for a good job to turn up – which might, besides providing him with a reasonable salary, enable him to escape from home. In the meantime he did jobs including farm work and clerking until he obtained a position as a teacher at a boys' school in Croydon, a working-class area of South London, just after his twenty-third birthday.

He started work in London in October 1908 and moved into *London* rooms in a family-run private house nearby. This was the first time he had lived away from home for any extended period, and working at the school proved extremely demanding, as he found it difficult to enforce discipline. However, in his leisure time he went up to central London to attend concerts and plays, and visited art galleries and bookshops. He continued his reading and writing, including further revisions to *Laetitia*.

Literary Breakthrough   Lawrence's breakthrough into the literary world came with some of his poems, which he sent initially to Jessie Chambers – still in Nottingham – for comment. Without his knowledge, she submitted them in September 1909 to Ford Madox Hueffer (later known as Ford Madox Ford), the illustrious critic and editor of the recently established radical journal *The English Review*. Hueffer decided to print a few of them and encouraged Lawrence to send him any further work of his, whatever the genre. Hueffer knew all the major London literati, and invited Lawrence to artistic gatherings where he met, among others, Wells, Yeats and Pound.

Because his journal pursued a radical line, Hueffer was especially interested in promoting Lawrence as an "author from the collieries", and suggested that Lawrence should write about the life of the people he was familiar with. Accordingly, Lawrence's first two plays, written around this period (*A Collier's Friday Night* and *The Widowing of Mrs Holroyd*), were concerned with the life of mining families and partly written in the Nottinghamshire dialect. In December 1910 he sent the manuscript of *Laetitia* to the London publisher Heinemann, accompanied by a letter of recommendation from Hueffer. Heinemann asked for some cuts and alterations – which Lawrence made, including renaming it *The White Peacock* – and accepted it for publication.

Love Life   Despite his efforts, Lawrence had failed to forge a physical relationship with any of his various female acquaintances. Around this time, he suggested to his long-time intellectual companion, Jessie Chambers – still living in Nottinghamshire – that they should become lovers. Jessie agreed, but Lawrence did not wish to be tied down by one woman, and the affair was extremely unhappy and bitter. In August 1911 the sexual side of the relationship ended, and two months later Lawrence's mother became seriously unwell, possibly with the first signs of the cancer that would ultimately kill her.

All the following year his mother was in increasingly severe pain, and he was now without Jessie. In this sense of isolation and sadness he embarked on the composition of a new novel, largely drawn from his own experiences at the time. He was at this period re-establishing contact with a friend from his adolescence, Louie Burrows, then living in Leicester. She was apparently not as intellectual as Jessie Chambers, but very loving and fond of Lawrence. Possibly on the rebound from Jessie Chambers, Lawrence proposed marriage to Louie.

Just at this time *The White Peacock* appeared in print, and Lawrence personally put the first copy of it into his mother's hands. His mother would die later that year, on 9th December.

Lawrence's second novel, entitled at this point *The Saga of Siegmund*, was rejected by Heinemann; they suggested numerous revisions and a change of title. Accordingly, Lawrence reworked the novel, which would appear as *The Trespasser* in 1912. At the same time as composing the later stages of *The Saga of Siegmund*, he had started on a third novel, which he planned to entitle *Paul Morel*. By now he had begun to realize his engagement to Louie had been a mistake – since she could not provide the lifelong intellectual companionship he desired – and agonized over ending their relationship. He became very depressed, and in November 1911 developed another severe, near-fatal case of pneumonia – which may have been an early symptom of the lung problems which would plague Lawrence throughout his entire life. He spent a month convalescing at a hotel in Bournemouth, making the final revisions to his second novel and progressing with *Paul Morel*. He gave up teaching on the advice of his doctors and returned to Eastwood in February 1912. There he completely rewrote *Paul Morel* – Jessie Chambers reading all his drafts and making suggestions – while living in his childhood home with his father and two sisters.

It was at this time that one of the major events of Lawrence's *Frieda* life occurred: he met the woman with whom he was to spend most of his life – Frieda Weekley, née von Richthofen – the daughter of minor German aristocrats from the Metz region. She was the wife of the Professor of Modern Languages at Nottingham University, Ernest Weekley, whom she had met and married at the age of nineteen. The couple lived in a respectable suburb of Nottingham with their three children. Lawrence first met her when in March 1912 he came to their house to enquire about the possibility of finding teaching work in Germany. He immediately fell passionately in love with her, even though she was eight years his senior. Since she reciprocated his feelings, he convinced her that she was wasting her best years in her current, comfortable way of life and persuaded her to start a relationship with him.

Travels and Writing   In May 1912 *The Trespasser* was published, to reasonably favourable reviews, and on the 12th of the same month Frieda left her husband and travelled with Lawrence to Metz. Ernest Weekley immediately asked for a divorce, stipulating that she should never see the children again. While in Germany staying with her relations, Lawrence made his final revision of *Paul Morel* and sent it off to Heinemann. The publisher rejected it as being poorly written and too sexually explicit. However, Edward Garnett, the reader for Duckworth publishers, assured Lawrence that if, under his guidance, he made a large number of alterations, he would recommend the novel for publication. Lawrence and Frieda undertook a walking tour of Germany, Austria and finally Italy, where they intended to stay for some months as it was much cheaper than Germany and they were short of money.

In Italy, in rooms near Gargnano, on Lake Garda, Lawrence made the requisite alterations to *Paul Morel*, renaming it *Sons and Lovers* in the process. He sent the novel off to Duckworth and, after further negotiations, the novel was accepted for publication. Lawrence now worked intensively on poems, plays and ideas for possible future novels, finally settling down to a project he provisionally entitled *The Sisters*, which would ultimately, over the next seven years, become *The Rainbow* and *Women in Love*. In June 1913, the couple finally returned to England, since Frieda desperately wanted to see her children again before consenting to a divorce which would forbid her access to them. *Sons and Lovers* had by this time been published to mixed but generally favourable reviews.

Frieda did not succeed in seeing her children, and was threatened with legal action if she attempted to do so again. The couple returned to Italy, this time to Lerici, near La Spezia. There Lawrence produced the first section of a completely revised version of *The Sisters* – which detailed the sexual relationships and emotional development of two sisters, Ella (later Ursula) and Gudrun Brangwen. Having sent this draft to Garnett – who lambasted it as very badly written – Lawrence set about a further revision. However, following the success of *Sons and Lovers*, other publishers were now making overtures to Lawrence, some offering him lucrative contracts for the novel – which by this time had been renamed *The Wedding Ring*. Garnett once again criticized the new version heavily, and in March Lawrence returned to London to negotiate a possible deal with another publisher: Methuen outbid Duckworth and were promised the novel. Finally, in April 1914, Frieda gained her divorce, and Lawrence married her in July of that year. Things seemed to be looking up on all fronts for Lawrence.

Then war broke out and the couple faced enormous *War and Rejection* problems in returning abroad. The War also hindered the possibility of getting further novels published, since there was a paper shortage, and the entire economy was now geared towards providing for the military effort. Furthermore, Frieda was regarded with suspicion because of her German origin. Lawrence – profoundly disillusioned with the War – felt that the conflict was barbaric and that the entire British national and racial consciousness had been polluted.

Suddenly Methuen returned the manuscript of *The Wedding Ring*, claiming the subject matter was too risqué, and that publishers' lists were being cut back drastically because of the War. Lawrence and Frieda were once again without money, so they moved to a small cottage in Chesham, Buckinghamshire. He rewrote *The Wedding Ring* between November 1914 and March 1915, splitting the novel into *The Rainbow* and what was ultimately to become *Women in Love*. However, *The Rainbow* became even more sexually explicit than the previously rejected drafts.

During these years, Lawrence had begun to enter new literary circles. Among others he had become acquainted with Lady Ottoline Morrell, the aristocratic society and artistic hostess. At her receptions he met famous intellectuals, such as E.M. Forster and Bertrand Russell. Lawrence's letters from 1914 and 1915 – principally to Russell – show the evolution of his ideas on the best way to live one's life and to develop one's real inner self. At first, Russell was highly impressed by Lawrence, but then became deeply disturbed by what he saw as the authoritarian character of his personality and beliefs, which he later characterized as "leading straight to Auschwitz".

The Rainbow was published in September 1915 and received *The Rainbow* vicious reviews. Bookstalls and libraries refused to stock it, *Controversy* because of what was perceived to be the pornographic nature of its material. Finally, in November 1915, the police seized all unsold copies and the book was prosecuted in the law courts for obscenity, the magistrates ordering all copies to be destroyed. Although some of Lawrence's artistic entourage protested against this censorship, it was generally the idea of censorship itself they were criticizing: most in fact detested the book as an aesthetic creation.

Move to Cornwall   Lawrence now seriously thought of emigrating permanently to America with Frieda to set up an artists' and writers' commune in Florida, encouraging their various acquaintances to come and join them. However, Lawrence could only acquire a passport if he declared himself ready to be summoned for military service at any time, which he could not bring himself to do. If they could not leave Britain, they decided to move as far from the centre of war activities in London as they could. Accordingly they hired a cottage in Cornwall, where they lived by growing their own vegetables, settling there in December 1915. In this cottage, Lawrence produced books of poetry and reminiscences of his time in Italy, as well as reviews and other pieces of writing that procured them a very meagre income. Although Lawrence was often ill with colds and pulmonary complaints – perhaps because of the winds from the sea and the moors – both he and Frieda enjoyed the open countryside and often entertained guests from London in their cottage.

Lawrence now began to recast the material left over from *The Wedding Ring*, using that work's original title, *The Sisters*, for the first draft of this reworking. After several revisions the manuscript went through the usual round of publishers, who all rejected it – one even asked if it was really finished. In addition to their reservations about the content, they were probably frightened off by Lawrence's reputation and the police prosecution of *The Rainbow*. Lady Ottoline Morrell had caught a glimpse of the manuscript, thought herself slandered in the person of the novel's society hostess Hermione, and consequently severed all ties with Lawrence.

Because of his weak lungs, Lawrence was rejected for conscription on medical grounds in June 1916, and the locals in Cornwall became suspicious and irritated at this noncombatant writer living with a German wife, and spread rumours that they were spies. They would sometimes be stopped by the coastguard while out on their walks, and return to their cottage to find it had been broken into and searched.

Return to London   In September 1917 they were finally served with a legal order
and Derbyshire   excluding them from Cornwall altogether, so they moved back
to London, staying in a series of cheap lodgings. In London

Lawrence attempted to settle down to writing his next novel, *Aaron's Rod*, but progress was slow due to their precarious living conditions and the fact that he was at the same time trying to eke out a living by writing poetry, reviews and essays. In May 1918, they moved back to the Midlands – to a cottage in Middleton-by-Wirksworth in Derbyshire – because it was so much cheaper to live there than in the south. Although he was now closer to his family, Lawrence felt himself to be "lost and exiled", sinking into severe depression and growing extremely pessimistic as to his future prospects.

In September 1918 Lawrence was compulsorily examined for military service: by this time the British Army was so desperate for manpower for the war effort that it was willing to conscript almost anybody. He was enlisted for "light non-military duties", a decision which drove him into a fury: "I've done with society and humanity. Labour and military can alike go to hell. Henceforth it is for myself, my own life, I live." He was never actually called up, since the War ended in November 1918. In February 1919 he went down with a serious bout of influenza, and nearly died – the disease was then killing millions of people worldwide.

The armistice meant that Lawrence and Frieda could finally *Leaving England* obtain passports, and they decided to abandon England for good. In December 1919 they moved to Capri, and then to Taormina in Sicily. Lawrence now concentrated on his work, *Psychoanalysis and the Unconscious*, followed by his next two novels, *The Lost Girl* and *Mr Noon*. *The Lost Girl* was published in Britain in November 1920 but, because of his reputation, many bookshops again refused to stock it. His publisher demanded both major revisions to this novel and further alterations to *Women in Love*, since the composer Philip Heseltine (better known by his pen name of Peter Warlock) had perceived himself as portrayed and libelled in the novel's character of Julian Halliday.

As a result of all this, the Lawrences grew utterly fed up *Australia and New* with Europe, and decided to renew their attempt at moving *Mexico* to the US, as Lawrence had been invited at this time to set up residence in Taos, a colony of writers and artists in New Mexico. Disillusioned with society, humanity and the artistic life, he and Frieda set off to the States. En route to New Mexico, they spent short periods in Ceylon and New Zealand, and six weeks in Australia, where Lawrence met the Australian writer Mollie Skinner, and collaborated with her in producing *The Boy in the Bush* – probably the least didactic of his novels and the one most similar to an ordinary adventure story. He also began to draft his next novel, *Kangaroo*, also based on Australian life. The couple finally arrived in San Francisco in August 1922, then making their way down to Taos, establishing themselves on a ranch on Lobo Mountain. Lawrence was overwhelmed by the primeval beauty of the landscape opening up around him. At Taos he completed *Kangaroo* and earned a slender living by journalism, reviews and a book of essays on American literature.

Mexico and Return to Europe In March 1923, Lawrence and Frieda visited Mexico and, by the lake near the settlement of Chapala in the south-west, Lawrence began work on his next novel, *The Plumed Serpent*, which dealt with pagan Mexican religion and political insurrection. Before taking up residence permanently in America, they decided to pay a brief visit to Europe, as Frieda in particular desperately wanted to see both her German and English families again. However, just before they were due to sail, the Lawrences had a huge row, the causes of which are unclear. Frieda sailed to Europe alone, and Lawrence returned to Mexico. It's possible that Frieda may have wanted to return to Europe permanently, whereas Lawrence detested the old Continent so wholeheartedly that he was determined this was going to be his last visit – the shorter the better.

Frieda did not return and, at the end of 1923, he finally wrote to her offering a separation, with the provision of a regular income. She begged him to return to Europe, and other old friends also expressed their desire to see him. Finally in November of that year he set off with the greatest reluctance. He wrote: "I don't want much to go to England – but I suppose it is the next move in the battle which never ends and which I never win." As soon as he reached England, he was confined to bed with a severe cold and, although he visited friends and relations, he declared openly that he now loathed London and the entire country. He once again appealed to friends to come back to America with him and set up an artists' and writers' commune, but only the artist Dorothy Brett would commit to doing so. At a farewell party, Lawrence drank too much and vomited over the meal table – this traumatic final event in England symbolizing all his loathing for European culture.

Lawrence, Frieda and Dorothy sailed back to the States *Return to America* in March 1924, and they all moved to a ranch just two miles away from their previous residence on Lobo Mountain. Unfortunately, his American publisher now went bankrupt, depriving him of a great deal of expected royalties. However, Lawrence at last seemed to have found some slight measure of happiness there, writing and living the simple life away from the civilization he so detested. The only major drawback was that he suffered from serious chest ailments, and began spitting blood – possibly as a result of the altitude of 2,600 metres. In Autumn 1924 came news that his father had died at the age of seventy-eight, but he did not return to Europe to attend the funeral.

In order to complete *The Plumed Serpent*, Lawrence *Tuberculosis* felt he needed to spend more time in Mexico to imbibe the atmosphere, so in October he, Frieda and Dorothy travelled down to Oaxaca, which seemed a warm paradise suited to the subject matter of the book and to sustained writing. However, tensions were now surfacing between Frieda and Dorothy, and Dorothy returned to America after just ten days. Lawrence finally finished the book in late January 1925, and immediately went down with a combination of influenza, typhoid and malaria which once again nearly cost him his life. Although he survived, his lungs were fatally damaged by these illnesses, and he was finally diagnosed with tuberculosis. He was given at most two years to live, and decided to return with Frieda to his ranch in the US. The doctor at the border initially refused Lawrence re-entry, as he now showed obvious signs of tuberculosis, a dangerous and contagious disease, but they were eventually granted a six-month residency.

Once back at the ranch, he recovered somewhat, and began writing again. In September 1925 – the six months having expired – the now forty-year-old Lawrence sailed back to Europe. The couple once again visited Lawrence's family, Frieda taking the opportunity to see her now adult children, before moving on through Germany and down to Italy, to a villa in Spotorno, a Ligurian town on the coast. Lawrence took up writing again, and started work in 1926 on his final novel, *Lady Chatterley's Lover*. Although Lawrence's health was generally stable, he still had bouts of blood-spitting, and felt his general condition slowly deteriorating. They then moved to a villa in Tuscany; Lawrence thought briefly of returning to

America, but realized that in his sick state he almost certainly would not be allowed entry, and that the strain of the long journey would exhaust his body still further.

Lady Chatterley's Lover   Lawrence was occupied with completing *Lady Chatterley's Lover* from October 1926 to summer 1928. The manuscript underwent countless radical alterations throughout these months, and during the final stages of revision, Lawrence was writing up to four thousand words a day. Although he had few hopes of its publication, because of its sexually explicit subject matter, he had discovered that it would be possible to publish the novel at his own expense on the Continent. 1,200 copies of the book, which he had arranged to be printed privately in Florence, finally appeared in June 1928. *Lady Chatterley's Lover* was an instant commercial success, and Lawrence for the first time in his life was relatively free from financial worries. After the publication of this novel, he decided to get away from the baking heat of Italy and live for a few months in the Swiss Alps, to see whether the mountain air would improve his condition. Although this change of environment benefited him somewhat, his coughing became more frequent, and he suffered increasingly severe haemorrhages. He tried not to let his illness defeat him, writing in a letter: "I feel so strongly as if my illness weren't really me – I feel perfectly well and all right, in myself. Yet there is this beastly torturing chest superimposed on me, and it's as if there was a demon lived there, triumphing, and extraneous to me." Frieda would later remark that she had never heard him complain about his health.

Last Days   With the money from *Lady Chatterley*, Lawrence and Frieda had some choice about where to live, and they selected a pleasant hotel in Bandol, on the French coast near Toulon. Lawrence tried to write newspaper articles and poems, but he could not undertake any further major projects, as his health was now deteriorating rapidly. He began to compose what would be his final work, *Apocalypse*: its purpose was to offer modern man a kind of psychic recovery of his connections with the old world, by providing a fresh view of humanity's "old, pagan vision" and the "pre-Christian heavens". But his physical condition by now was very poor, and he finally agreed to enter the Ad Astra sanatorium in Vence, near Nice. There he grew very despondent, and decided to discharge himself, as he wanted to die on his own terms. He and Frieda rented a villa in Vence, and hired nurses to look after him. On Sunday

2nd March 1930 his condition worsened considerably; he admitted he needed morphine, and a doctor administered the drug. Lawrence died that evening. Frieda wrote that he was buried "in the little cemetery of Vence which looks over the Mediterranean that he cared so much about". In 1935 his body was exhumed and cremated, and a chapel was erected near his second ranch in the mountains overlooking Taos to house his ashes.

D.H. Lawrence's Works

D.H. Lawrence wrote his first novel, *The White Peacock*, under *The White Peacock* various working titles, between 1906 and 1910. As mentioned above, the London publisher William Heinemann accepted it for publication, and the book came out in 1911. The novel follows a first-person narrator, Cyril Beardsall, who is continually questioning his identity and his place in the world – even at this stage of Lawrence's career, his writing probes the question of the alienation of modern humanity from its natural roots and instincts. The setting is the countryside around Nottingham (Beardsall, incidentally, was the maiden name of Lawrence's mother).

Cyril and his sister Lettie have had a conventional middle-class upbringing: they are cultured and artistic, but they are dissatisfied with their life, and the novel deals with their failure to find genuine love. Cyril courts Emily Saxton, a farmer's daughter, who ends up marrying somebody else, while Lettie, although deeply in love with Emily's brother George, makes a conventional marriage to a narrow-minded man of a much higher social rank. Following this rejection, George marries a pub landlord's daughter, which leaves him unfulfilled, and he becomes an apathetic alcoholic.

There is one further major character, who represents the rejection of modern culture and civilization and embodies the return to nature and the instincts. This is Frank Annable, who had been a student at Cambridge University before becoming a vicar and marrying a local aristocrat, Lady Crystabel. He has rejected his former life and is now a gamekeeper on a large estate, living in the woods with a second wife and a large family. He is generally disliked by the local men, apparently because, with his animal vitality, he has a great deal of success with their wives. Cyril is attracted by his superb physique and personality, but Annable is found dead at the bottom of a quarry – it is not certain whether he has slipped or been pushed in by a gang of locals. It is interesting to note that, in his very last novel, *Lady Chatterley's Lover*, written around twenty years later, earthiness and return to one's natural instincts are also represented by a gamekeeper who has rejected his middle-class educated background.

George and Lettie therefore are left at the end of the novel feeling that they have not managed to unite their alienated artistic nature with the innate animal instinctive level of their own humanity; neither have they succeeded in bonding at any meaningful level with the members of the human race who are much more attuned with these instincts than they are.

The Trespasser   The follow-up to *The White Peacock* was composed between March 1910 and February 1912. It was originally to be titled *The Saga of Siegmund*, but was finally published in 1912 as *The Trespasser*. Mainly set on the Isle of Wight, with other scenes in north and south London and Cornwall, the novel centres on Siegmund MacNair, an orchestral musician and music teacher, who is married, with five children, to Beatrice. Despite his domestic comforts, he is restless and gets involved in a relationship with one of his pupils, Helena Verden. The bulk of the novel deals with the week they spend together on the Isle of Wight. The relationship does not work on a physical level: he is passionately attracted to her, but she is very withdrawn. Siegmund, in despair at all the conflicts and tensions in his life, hangs himself, and his wife, for the children's sake, deliberately suppresses all memory of him. But something has died within Helena Verden after this tragedy: she has entered a deep period of emotional stasis, and the novel ends with her new friend and possible future lover, Cecil, trying desperately to arouse her from this state.

Sons and Lovers   Around the same time *The Trespasser* was written, Lawrence was working on another manuscript, provisionally entitled *Paul Morel*, which was completed in 1912 and published as *Sons and Lovers* in 1913. It incorporates numerous elements of Lawrence's life. The "Bestwood" of the novel is the author's home village of Eastwood, and the Morel family bears many resemblances to his own. The novel charts the protagonist Paul Morel's sexual, emotional and intellectual development from his childhood up to the age of twenty-five. The first part of the novel is devoted to a recreation of the early married life and environment of Paul's parents. Like Lawrence's own family, the father is a miner who drinks, while the mother is intellectual, artistic and well informed; this leads to inevitable arguments. Paul shares his mother's artistic nature and becomes strongly attached to her. Following the early death of his brother from illness, Paul too nearly dies at the age of sixteen and, from then on, the novel concerns Paul's developing emotional and sexual relationships, and his attempt to become independent in all ways from his mother. He has done exceptionally well at school and wishes to become an artist, but, during the period covered by the novel, works as a clerk at a local factory. At the age of sixteen, he meets his first love, Miriam, who bears many resemblances to Jessie Chambers. They are both passionate about art and ideas, and very much in love, but the sexual side of their relationship is fraught with difficulties. Paul feels he is betraying his mother, while Miriam at first does not want to involve herself in sex outside marriage. Paul constantly tries to force the issue, and Miriam finally acquiesces unwillingly, feeling she is making a great sacrifice for him. This turns out to be a disastrous experience, and Paul ends their relationship. He then enters on a brief and much more fulfilling relationship with an older married woman, but she finally decides to remain faithful to her husband. Near the end of the novel, Paul's mother dies, and he is left on the threshold of his maturity alone, but having become much more aware of his own identity.

The extremely convoluted gestation of Lawrence's next novel, *The Rainbow*, should be studied with that of the subsequent work, *Women in Love*, since they are both developments of what was originally planned as one novel. *The Rainbow* was published just two years after the commencement of the first draft, in 1913, but the reworking of the later material as a second volume, *Women in Love*, took until 1920. The preliminary drafts were written between March 1913 and August 1915. The first draft, under the provisional title *The Sisters,* was written between March and June 1913. A complete revision, still with the same provisional title, took place between August 1913 and January 1914. This was then substantially revised again, under the new title *The Wedding Ring*, from February to May 1914, and Lawrence finally took the decision to split the material into two books. The first, now known as *The Rainbow*, was put together between November 1914 and March 1915, and

The Rainbow

published in September 1915. The book portrays the earlier generations of the Nottinghamshire family whose modern members are treated at length in *Women in Love*. The setting is mainly the industrial counties of Nottinghamshire and its neighbour Derbyshire. Tom Brangwen, a young Midlands farmer, marries a Polish exile, Lydia Lensky, in 1867, when he is twenty-eight and she is thirty-four. Lydia is more cultured and intellectual than Tom, and the novel explores firstly the tensions in their marriage, and the way their relationship gradually evolves into a harmonious loving partnership. The couple live with Lydia's daughter, Anna, by her first marriage to a Polish revolutionary. We are shown Anna's development to maturity, until she finally marries Will Brangwen, the son of Tom's brother Alfred. Their stormy marriage is depicted in detail and, although they ultimately achieve some sort of harmony, the relationship is not as happy as Anna's parents, but represents more of a compromise. One of the major differences is in religion: Anna is a "pagan", in that she worships nature and the instinctive physical life, whereas Will is a Christian mystic, hankering after experiences of the eternal and absolute.

The major part of the novel is taken up with the third generation of this family, and mainly describes the life of Will and Anna's daughter, Ursula Brangwen. She is profoundly conscious of her responsibility to form her own personality, and to gain independence from her early upbringing and family; she questions her father's Christianity, and has various romantic relationships, including a lesbian affair. She trains as a student teacher, later becoming a passionate critic of contemporary industrial society and of the alienation of the natural instincts from everyday life. She becomes engaged to a young soldier, Anton Skrebensky, but she gradually opens her eyes to his conventionality and adherence to social norms. She breaks off their relationship and he, unbeknown to her, marries another woman and is posted on military service to India. Ursula discovers she is pregnant by him, and writes to him asking for marriage after all. However, before receiving an answer, she is involved in a traumatic incident while out walking, becomes dangerously ill and suffers a miscarriage. This leads her to a period of epiphany, self-discovery and rebirth; she is delighted when she learns that Skrebensky is already married, realizing that she must wait for the right man "created by God" to come along. She glimpses a rainbow, and has a vision of a new reality for the whole of society, which will enable it to grow once more from its organic roots, and throw off the shackles of industrialization.

When Lawrence had reworked *The Rainbow* to his satis- *Women in Love* faction and sent it off to the publisher, he comprehensively recast the remaining material, between April and June 1916, into a new narrative, and resurrected for it the former title *The Sisters*. Between July 1916 and January 1917 this was once again rewritten drastically, and given the new title *Women in Love* (this first version of the novel has since been published as *The First Women in Love*). Unfortunately, by this time *The Rainbow* had been prosecuted for obscenity and all unsold copies withdrawn and destroyed by a legal ruling. Lawrence submitted the manuscript of his new novel to various publishers, including Duckworth, Constable and Secker, and they all rejected it, commenting that, in the present climate of public opinion, with Lawrence's reputation, it would be unpublishable without drastic revision. Furthermore, several of Lawrence's acquaintances who had seen the manuscript claimed to perceive themselves satirized in its text. Accordingly, Lawrence, presumably fearing not only another prosecution for obscenity but libel suits into the bargain, rethought the entire project, and radically reworked *Women in Love* over the two years between March 1917 and September 1919. The novel was first published in June 1921, and then further significant changes were made to the second edition, to produce *Women in Love* as it is now generally known.

The novel traces the adventures of the Ursula Brangwen of *The Rainbow*, now aged twenty-six, and a teacher at a grammar school. She is the lover of Rupert Birkin, an articulate school inspector who has sufficient private means to be able to retire if he so wishes. Ursula's sister Gudrun is twenty-five, has completed a course at art college and teaches at the same school; she is extremely self-confident and dresses in a bright and bohemian fashion. Gudrun's lover is Gerald Crich, who is around thirty and the son of a wealthy colliery owner. He is handsome, blond, physically active and in charge of the colliery. However, he lacks a sense of any deep meaning in his life, and his relationship with Gudrun runs into the sands because, rather than striving to achieve a mutual unity of their two personalities, he needs constant reassurances of her affections.

The novel may be said to explore love and sexual relationships in both their creative and destructive aspects. Rupert Birkin contains both of these opposites within himself. He despairs of the modern industrial world and of the human race; however, he refuses to surrender to cynicism and apathy, but persists in his belief in personal fulfilment and integration through interpersonal relationships. These relationships will form the bedrock of a new, organic society, not distorted by over-intellectualism or industrialization. Birkin is, in fact, largely a self-portrait of Lawrence. Like Lawrence, he believes that throughout history the human race has either experienced periods of creative progress or of disintegration. With industrialization and the War, the world is currently, according to him, in a "destructive" cycle. Most of the characters throughout the novel display various degrees of over-intellectualism and alienation from the natural world and from their instincts. Birkin is at the beginning of the novel involved in a relationship with the wealthy aristocrat Hermione Roddice, who is described as "a medium for the culture of ideas" – that is, entirely locked up inside her own head, and cut off from her instincts. Not surprisingly, the relationship collapses. However, the liaison between Gerald and Gudrun is purely sensual, and is ultimately just as unfulfilling. In the end, Ursula and Birkin both resign from their jobs, marry and retire to the Continent – presumably having enough money to do so from Rupert's private income. Their relationship appears to be developing into an integrated and harmonious success. However, Gerald and Gudrun's sensual affair has gone off the rails; she has despairingly taken another lover and, in the Austrian Tyrol, he attempts to strangle her and then flees into the snows in a deliberate suicide attempt.

The Lost Girl   Eight months before *Women in Love* came off the press, D.H. Lawrence completed *The Lost Girl*, a novel he had begun composing as early as December 1912, and which had also undergone several rewrites and title changes. It was eventually published in November 1920.

The novel traces the history of the main protagonist, Alvina Houghton, the "lost girl" of the title, from the age of twenty-three to thirty-two. She is the daughter of well-to-do tradespeople in Woodhouse, a fictional mining town based on Eastwood. Initially, she is "lost" because she seems destined to end up as an old maid, but subsequently she becomes "lost" to those around her because of her rebellion against her conventional upbringing: she plans to move to Australia with her lover, and then, on being talked out of this, moves to north London to train as a maternity nurse, where she gains first-hand experience of the poverty of the capital's slums. On her return to Woodhouse, she finds that no one can afford to hire her services as a nurse on a private basis, and so abandons the idea of earning a living in this manner for the time being. She toys with the idea of marrying various rich men, but decides they are all too cold and inhuman. At the age of thirty, after her father's death, she joins a travelling theatre group, which contains a number of dark passionate foreigners, whom she feels drawn to but ultimately rejects. Leaving the itinerant actors, she takes up her former occupation as a maternity nurse again and becomes engaged to an older wealthy doctor. However, she breaks off this engagement, marries the Italian Ciccio – who was part of her former theatre group – and moves to the mountains of Italy with him. Ciccio is called up for military service, and the novel ends with Alvina, now pregnant, having to bear and bring up a child alone. She is once more lost in an alien environment from which she feels cut off.

Aaron's Rod, a novel which Lawrence had written between October 1917 and November 1921, was published in England in 1922. Aaron Sisson is a mine worker and secretary of the local miners' union in Beldover – again modelled on Eastwood – and also a talented musician, principally on the flute and piccolo. He had originally trained to be a teacher, but he ultimately decided he preferred manual labour. At the age of thirty-three, having inherited a substantial amount of money from his recently deceased mother, he leaves his wife and three children well provided for, and sets off to London on a journey of self-discovery. There he becomes an orchestral musician and frequents intellectual and artistic circles. He is seduced by a scheming female acquaintance, but decides that this is not the type of relationship he left his family for. He falls into depression and succumbs to severe physical illness. The writer Rawdon Lilly, a "freak" and "outsider" by his own description, nurses him back to health, and reinforces Aaron's sense of revulsion at modern marriage, and his fear of being entrapped therein. Aaron goes back to see his wife, who not surprisingly is extremely bitter, and so he leaves for Italy at an invitation from Rawdon. There he has a passionate relationship with a

Aaron's Rod

91

noble Italian woman, from which Aaron once again distances himself, because he wants to withdraw still deeper into himself and avoid being tied down. The novel ends with Rawdon helping Aaron to accept his intuition that the "love urge" has been exhausted by civilization, and that the new creative urge is that of a power surging from the deepest reaches of the soul, which must be used to renew civilization.

Kangaroo   As mentioned, from June to July 1922, while he was in Australia, Lawrence wrote the bulk of a novel, *Kangaroo*, set around Sydney, which was later published in 1923.

The novel is about Richard Somers and his wife Harriett, who have come to Australia to start a new life after becoming disillusioned with Europe. Their neighbours, Jack and Victoria Callcott, turn out to be members of a clandestine paramilitary organization planning to seize political power by force. Jack offers Somers the chance to become a member, and takes him to see the leader of the movement, Benjamin Cooley, usually referred to as "Kangaroo". Cooley advocates love and brotherhood, but all within a strictly hierarchical model of society controlled by one all-powerful leader. Somers, although in essence sympathetic to his cause, is sceptical and will not commit himself, while Harriett is resentful of her husband's attraction to Kangaroo and the organization. Somers then becomes interested in socialism, but is equally sceptical: Kangaroo's organization is based on love organized through power, whereas the socialists' ideals are based on love for humanity as a generalized and abstract concept, without taking the individual into account. Neither system is what Somers believes he, or humanity in general, needs on a personal level. He is present when the socialists and the right-wingers fight at a rally and numerous men are killed. Kangaroo is wounded, and Somers goes to visit him. Kangaroo asks him once and for all to dedicate himself to the movement, but Somers cannot bring himself to do this. Kangaroo dies, and Somers and his wife start to consider moving to America. Before he leaves, Somers declares that he can only commit himself to nature, to "non-human gods, non-human human being".

The Boy in the Bush   Having met the author Mollie Skinner in Australia, Lawrence collaborated on a novel with her, *The Boy and the Bush*, which was published in 1924. Although both names appear on the title page, the precise degree of each author's contribution is unclear. It relates the story of Jack

Grant, who arrives in Australia from England in 1882 at the age of eighteen, after having been expelled from school and agricultural college, and involved in various other dubious doings. The novel depicts how he becomes a successful sheep-farmer and gold-miner by his early twenties. There is little of the didacticism and pretentiousness of Lawrence's other novels, and it is in essence an uncomplicated adventure story.

Lawrence turned to Mexico for the setting of his next novel, *The Plumed Serpent*, which he wrote on location in order to immerse himself fully in the country's atmosphere and accustom himself to the mores of the indigenous population. He completed the novel in 1925 and it was published in England the following year. In *The Plumed Serpent* a revolutionary movement in Mexico intends to overthrow Christianity and re-establish worship of the old gods, such as Quetzalcoatl – the "plumed serpent" of the title. The leaders of this movement even assume the names of these old gods. Kate Leslie, an Irish widow of around forty who is visiting Mexico, is at first impressed by the animal pagan vigour of the organization, but then becomes suspicious of its mysticism and barbarity. The novel simultaneously charts the progress of the movement and Kate's fluctuating sympathies towards it. The movement comes to control large swathes of the country, but Kate grows increasingly alienated by its inhumanity. However, she cannot resist the pagan "soul power" of one of the revolutionary leaders who has named himself Quetzalcoatl, and she agrees to participate in a ritual marriage with him. But even after the ceremony she is profoundly dubious, and at the end of the novel we are left wondering whether the movement will be crushed and whether she will become utterly disillusioned and try to withdraw from it.

Lady Chatterley's Lover was Lawrence's final and most successful major novel. It was written between 1926 and 1928: during this time he completed three separate versions, each of which were subsequently published. The third and final version, the only one to appear in Lawrence's lifetime, was privately printed first in Florence in 1928 and then in Paris the following year. In Britain, due to the book's controversial content, it was only published by Secker in a radically expurgated version in February 1932. The first British unexpurgated printing, by Penguin in August 1960, was prosecuted for obscenity; following the collapse of the case, it

The Plumed Serpent

Lady Chatterley's Lover

93

went on general sale in November of that year, becoming an instant best-seller. The first version of the novel, composed between late 1926 and early 1927, was first published by Dial Press in New York with a preface by Frieda Lawrence. The second version, written immediately after the first one, was not published in English until 1972, when Heinemann issued it under the title of *John Thomas and Lady Jane*, although an Italian translation was published by Arnoldo Mondadori as early as 1954.

The final version has its setting in Eastwood and other Nottinghamshire towns, as well as Sheffield and Chesterfield – with brief scenes in Venice and London. Its protagonist is Connie Reid, who has had a wealthy, artistic and unconventional upbringing. She and her elder sister Hilda are allowed a great deal of freedom, and both have had sexual relationships by the time they are eighteen. At the beginning of the First World War they settle briefly in London and become part of a coterie of university intellectuals. Hilda marries, and Connie forms an attachment with Clifford Chatterley – a shy and nervous young aristocrat, who had been studying at Cambridge at the outbreak of war, but then joined the army – marrying him in 1917 when he is home on leave. Clifford is seriously wounded in battle, and becomes sexually impotent. Following the deaths of relatives, he becomes heir to the family title and estate. Clifford is not only impotent, but seriously depressed, and takes up writing as a therapy, eventually becoming a successful author. He plays host to gatherings of literati and other intellectuals, and Connie begins to feel more and more empty, frustrated and peripheral. In 1924, when she is twenty-seven, she sees the gamekeeper Mellors (known as Parkin in the second version) washing his naked body in the woods, and feels herself flaming back into life. She and Mellors become lovers, and they both rediscover their deep inner selves and connection with nature. Mellors is in fact an educated man who has rejected his middle-class upbringing to revert to a more meaningful working life. Therefore, though he can discourse on intellectual subjects, and can speak with a refined accent, he prefers to talk in broad dialect, and to project a working-class persona. He too, before he met Connie, had become sad and isolated, disillusioned by the War and the destruction of nature by industrialization. He has previously had various loveless affairs with women, including a now estranged wife.

However, his liaison with Connie removes all his encrusted bitterness. Connie becomes pregnant, and at the end of the novel they are both waiting for divorces so that they can marry, live on a farm and start a new life together, sheltered from the artificiality they see around them.

Mr Noon is an unfinished novel in two parts, which Lawrence *Mr Noon* wrote between 1920 and 1922. Secker posthumously published the first part in 1934, at the end of a collection of Lawrence's short stories, and fifty years later the Cambridge University Press edition appeared, including the very incomplete second part. The novel relates the past life of Gilbert Noon, a science teacher at a school in Nottinghamshire. It is revealed that he came from a working-class background, but proved to be so brilliant at maths, science and music that he gained a scholarship to go to Cambridge University, becoming one of the most outstanding mathematicians of the age. However, due to his somewhat dissipated lifestyle, he did not manage to progress up the academic ladder, and so returned home and became a teacher. He is caught in the act of having sex with Emmie Bostock, a twenty-three-year-old schoolteacher and, upon her apparently becoming pregnant, he is forced to resign his teaching post. In the second part of the novel Gilbert roams around Germany and elopes with a married woman over the Alps into Italy, where he feels himself to be "reborn" – at which point the fragment ends.

During the course of his life, Lawrence issued twelve vol- *Other Works* umes of poetry and had scores of poems published in journals. He produced three collections of short stories and six novellas, as well as a large number of stories published in magazines which were not collected during his lifetime. He also wrote seven plays, and his prolific non-fiction includes volumes on psychoanalysis and philosophy, travel sketches and hundreds of reviews and articles for the press.

The Fox was first published along with 'The Captain's Doll' *The Fox* and 'The Ladybird' under the title *The Ladybird* in 1923.

The novella is set in 1919 on an abandoned farmstead. Working on the farmstead are two women in their twenties – March and Banford. Their relationship is ambiguously characterized – it's possible they are lesbian lovers, but we never know for sure. Lawrence uses elements of masculinity in his portrayal of them – for instance, March habitually wears the uniform of a land girl, and a scene in which she adopts a more traditionally feminine dress sparks a revelation in the character of Henry.

March and Banford struggle to make a living from their work on the farm, and one particular problem facing them is that of a fox who continually steals their chickens. One day, March sees the fox and, looking into its eyes, is entranced by its gaze. There's something almost supernatural about the encounter, and the fox preys on March's mind from that point onwards.

A Cornish soldier called Henry arrives on the farm. He used to live there with his grandfather, and he persuades the women to allow him to stay there. From the start, he is seen by March as having a mysterious resemblance to the fox – almost, in some sense, being the fox. She becomes awkward in his presence.

Henry makes himself at home on the farm, and hatches a scheme to marry March in order to obtain possession of the farm for himself. He is aware that he has a strange power over March, as the fox does. He asks her to marry him, and she agrees, although she doesn't love him. This causes problems between her and Banford, who is deeply distressed at the possibility of March marrying Henry, and does her best to prevent it. Nevertheless, Henry manages to secure a promise of marriage from March. He then leaves to rejoin his regiment. While he is away, March sends him a letter breaking off the engagement. This makes him furious. For him, it is no longer about securing the farm – it is proposed that they emigrate to Canada after their marriage; by now he has strong possessive desires towards March. He leaves his regiment and returns to the farm. He now hates Banford for swaying March away from marrying him. When he arrives back, he contrives for a tree to fall on her, killing her.

Having lost Banford, March marries Henry. But neither of them are happy. The novella ends with them contemplating their future in Canada.

Screen Adaptations

Most of Lawrence's novels – including such lesser-known ones as *The Boy in the Bush* and *Kangaroo* – and a number of his short stories have been filmed either for television or cinema. Although the earliest of these date from the late 1940s, they were all substantially expurgated until the late 1960s, when a more liberal social climate began to allow more explicit imagery and language in films and stage plays. D.H. Lawrence's outlook chimed with that of the new generation, as attested by the 1969 cult classic *Easy Rider*, in which an alcoholic failed lawyer played by Jack Nicholson immediately opens a bottle on his release from prison for drunk and disorderly behaviour with the words: "To ol' D.H. Lawrence". On their way across America, the film's two protagonists, played by Peter Fonda and Dennis Hopper, visit a commune reminiscent of Taos, where Lawrence spent some time, and the film implies that Lawrence was in some way a forerunner of the permissive and sexually liberated Sixties.

The Fox has been filmed once, in 1967. The screenplay was written by Lewis John Carlino and Howard Koch. It was the directorial debut of Mark Rydell, and starred Sandy Dennis, Anne Heywood and Keir Dullea. The film shifts the action of the novella to Canada in the Sixties, and portrays Banford and March explicitly as lesbians. It was critically well received, winning nominations for the Golden Globe and Academy Awards.

Select Bibliography

Standard Edition
The most authoritative edition of *The Fox* is included in the Cambridge University Press volume *The Fox, The Captain's Doll, The Ladybird*, edited by Dieter Mehl (Cambridge: Cambridge University Press, 2002).

Biographies:
Aldington, Richard, *Portrait of a Genius, but...: A Biography of D.H. Lawrence* (London: Heinemann, 1950)
Meyers, Jeffrey, *D.H. Lawrence: A Biography* (London: Macmillan, 1990)
Moore, Harry Thornton, *The Priest of Love: A Life of D.H. Lawrence*, 2nd ed. (London: Heinemann, 1974)
Nehls, Edward, ed., *D.H. Lawrence: A Composite Biography* (Madison, WI: University of Wisconsin Press, 1959)
Sagar, Keith, *The Life of D.H. Lawrence: An Illustrated Biography* (London: Eyre Methuen: 1980)
Squires, Michael and Talbot, Lynn K., *Living at the Edge: A Biography of D.H. Lawrence and Frieda von Richthofen* (London: Robert Hale, 2002)

Worthen, John, *D.H. Lawrence: The Early Years 1885–1912* (Cambridge: Cambridge University Press, 1991)
Worthen, John, *D.H. Lawrence: The Life of an Outsider* (London: Allen Lane, 2005)

Additional Background Material:
Boulton, James T., ed., *The Selected Letters of D.H. Lawrence* (Cambridge: Cambridge University Press, 1997)
Miller, Henry, *The World of Lawrence: A Passionate Appreciation* (London: Calder, 1985)
Poplawski, Paul, *D.H. Lawrence: A Reference Companion* (Westport, CT & London: Greenwood Press, 1996)

On the Web:
www.nottingham.ac.uk/mss/online/dhlawrence